Praise for The David

"I can only applaud the rep[rint of the?]
Dave Brandstetter books. I'[...]
the phrase '*an important wri[ter*...]
but if one's going to use the label, [Hansen is no?]
unreasonable bearer of it."

—**Lawrence Block**

"Incredible books, much overlooked."

—**Jeff Abbott**

"The Brandstetter books are classics of the private eye
genre … It's great to see them available again."

—**Peter Robinson**

"First published over fifty years ago now, Hansen's novels
are not just clever and compelling stories, but to my mind
they are also a feat of incredible bravery. I wish I'd
discovered him sooner."

—**Russ Thomas, CrimeReads**

"Hansen is one of the best we have … [He] knows how to
tell a tough, unsentimental, fast-moving story in an
exceptionally urbane literary style."

—*New York Times Book Review*

"After forty years, Hammett has a worthy successor."

—*The Times* (**London**)

"Mr. Hansen is an excellent craftsman, a compelling writer."
—*The New Yorker*

"Apart from its virtues as fiction, Hansen's *Early Graves* is
a field correspondent's breathtaking dispatch from a
community in the midst of disaster."

—*Time*

"Read in the order written, [the Brandstetter mysteries] are remarkably linked through symbol, incident, and character, to the point that one sees them as a single, multi-volume novel, by which one may learn a great deal about what it means to be homosexual and male in modern America."

—*The New Republic*

"Hansen is quite simply the most exciting and effective writer of the classic California private-eye novel working today."

—*Los Angeles Times*

"No one in the history of the detective novel has had the daring to do what Joseph Hansen has done: make his private eye a homosexual ... who is both a first-rate investigator and one of the most interesting series characters in the history of the genre."

—**David Geherin,**
The American Private Eye

"The first thing I ever read by Joseph Hansen was *Fadeout* (1970). It's the seminal novel in a mystery series about a smart, tough, uncompromising insurance investigator by the name of David Brandstetter. He is a Korean War vet and ruggedly masculine. He's educated, principled, compassionate—but willing and able to use violence when nothing else works. He represents the (then) new breed of PI—the post-World War II private investigator. There are no bottles of rye in Dave's desk, there are no sleazy secrets in his past, and the dames don't much tend to throw themselves at him. He is neither tarnished nor afraid. Oh, and one other thing. He's gay. ... He was not the first gay detective to hit mainstream crime fiction, but he was the first normal gay detective, and that—as the poet said —has made all the difference."

—**Josh Lanyon,**
from *The Golden Age of Gay Fiction*

EARLY GRAVES

THE DAVE BRANDSTETTER NOVELS

Fadeout (1970)
Death Claims (1973)
Troublemaker (1975)
The Man Everybody Was Afraid Of (1978)
Skinflick (1979)
Gravedigger (1982)
Nightwork (1984)
The Little Dog Laughed (1986)
Early Graves (1987)
Obedience (1988)
The Boy Who Was Buried This Morning (1990)
A Country of Old Men (1991)

EARLY GRAVES

JOSEPH HANSEN

A DAVE BRANDSTETTER NOVEL

SYNDICATE BOOKS
NEW YORK

First published in 1987
by The Mysterious Press

This edition published in 2023
by Syndicate Books
www.syndicatebooks.com

Distributed by
Soho Press, Inc.
227 W 17th Street
New York, NY 10011

ISBN 978-1-68199-063-7
eISBN 978-1-68199-064-4

Printed in the United States of America

10 9 8 7 6 5 4 3 2 1

In memory of Wayne Placek
Music, and lights, and laughter, And after these, the dark . . .

HE CROSSED AIRPORT tarmac in the rain, and climbed a cold, wet steel staircase to a DC-8. He had been waiting for this. Six days in Fresno were plenty. The death claims division of Sequoia Life had been right in their suspicions. They had hired him to find proof that what looked like death by accident in a fire at a small printing plant had been murder. The wife had killed the husband for his insurance. But digging out the proof had been slow going.

The aircraft smelled stale inside. Freshener sprayed through the ducts was trying to dispel the spent breath and smoke and body warmth of the load of passengers who had just gotten off, but the crowd boarding with him was bringing new smells of rain-damp clothing. He stowed attaché case and raincoat in an overhead compartment, then settled into a window seat and buckled his belt. The seat was in the non-smoking section. He was trying to quit.

The plane sat for half an hour by the terminal, and another twenty minutes out on a runway. Dave looked up from the pages of the in-flight magazine, now and then to gaze off at the rainy outline of the Sierras looming to the east. The plane lifted off, rain hissing against the small windows, at 10:40 A.M., and touched down in the rain at

LAX at 11:25, so there was still something left of the day. Standing, waiting, at the luggage-go-round, he forgot and lit a cigarette, then remembered and dropped it and put a foot on it.

Outside, under a massive gray concrete overhang, he stood on cement, attaché case and grip at his feet, the raincoat hung over his shoulders because it was cold and damp as a tomb here. He watched cab drivers and airport cops scream at each other, watched jitneys stop and take on hotel-bound arrivals, watched passenger cars jockey for spaces at the curbs. Finally he saw Cecil's flame-painted van, glossy with rain, picked up the bags, jogged to where it waited for him, the horns of twenty cars clamoring behind it. Cecil leaned across, opened the door, grabbed the bags, dumped them into the back of the van. Dave climbed in and slammed the door. Cecil gave him a kiss, put the van in gear, they moved on, and the honking stopped—most of it. They inched along for a time in bumper-to-bumper traffic, then were on a broad, curving stretch of roadway swinging past looming glass and metal buildings, office complexes, hotels. Then they were on a boulevard and pointed northward. And Cecil said, "I was glad to get your call. Those taxi drivers, from what I hear, they'll take you for every dime before they let you out at home. Drive you to Northridge, just to run up the meter."

"Tell me about it," Dave said. "Thanks for coming."

Cecil stared ahead past the swinging windshield wipers that pushed aside the rain, pushed aside the rain, pushed aside the rain. Red traffic lights glowed at a broad intersection. He braked the van, glanced at Dave, and said, "I'll come anytime you ask, anywhere. You know that."

Dave nodded curtly. "I know that."

"All you have to do"—Cecil moved the gearshift lever—"is ask." The signal switched to go. He moved the van on across the intersection, and started it up a long slope 'tween green hills where abandoned oil pumps rusted in the rain. "I keep waiting for you to ask." He was a tall, gangly, good-

2

looking black who worked as a field reporter in television news. He was twenty-five years old. Dave had met him on a case up the central coast a few years back. Later they had settled in together in Dave's house. And worked together. Until Cecil had been shot almost to death, until Cecil had been forced to kill a man to save Dave's life. After that he had gone back to the newsroom. Tried. But another case had forced him to help out again. He was smart and resourceful and had got Dave out of trouble.

But he had made trouble for himself. It was still not over.

"You want to come back?" Dave said. "Come back. You were the one who left. It wasn't my idea."

"It was your idea to take Chrissie in," Cecil said.

"It was your idea to marry her." Dave lit a cigarette with shaking hands. "I only wanted to shelter her till things could be worked out by the courts."

"The courts." Cecil stopped himself, pressed his mouth tight, drew in air through his nose. The van topped the long rise, and below lay the west side of the city, stretching miles in the rain, under tattered clouds, mountains off to the north, shrouded in mist. Cecil said, keeping tight control over his voice, "Did anybody ever tell you, you have ice water in your veins?"

"Several people." Dave blew away smoke, groped for and found the ashtray in the blue dash. "On several occasions. Always when they knew I was right and they were wrong. Emotions doesn't change facts. And they hated believing that."

"I've told you from the start, it wasn't emotion," Cecil said. "Her father was dead, murdered, the only one who loved and cared for her. Her grandmother wouldn't have let her come to harm, but she was dead, too. Her damned mother wanted to control her so she could control all that money Chrissie had coming. You know what her mother is. Her mother's boyfriend tried to rape Chrissie. The County wanted to put her in a foster home. Somebody had to do something."

"You've told me," Dave said.

"It was a cool, calculated decision," Cecil said. "No emotion involved. Except yours. It only took a day to drive her to Las Vegas and marry her, so she'd be her own boss, and nobody could rip her off. She's blind, Dave. She's only seventeen years old, for Christ sake."

"And that day," Dave said, "was the first day of the rest of your life—right?"

"No way." Cecil shook his head hard. "Dave, she'll get over it. It's a teenage infatuation. She'll get tired of me and ask out." He braked the van behind a long line of rain-washed cars at the foot of the grade. "Not the rest of my life—no."

"Yes—unless you tell her. You should never have let her take you to bed. You've got brains that absolutely stagger me. How could you be so stupid?"

"She was sad and lost and alone in the dark," Cecil said. "She needed somebody to hold her."

"And you think she's going to get tired of that?"

"You did," Cecil said. "You shut me right out."

"It was your decision, not mine," Dave said. "You are the dearest thing in life to me. You're bright and funny and gentle and decent and full of life. And I will never get tired of you, and neither will Chrissie. It's not up to her anyway. You're the adult. Tell her the truth—that it was an act of kindness that got out of hand."

"I can't hurt her like that," Cecil said.

"It will hurt more the longer you let it go on."

"Dave, she needs somebody who gives a damn."

"And sex is the only way to convey that?" Dave asked.

"It beats gin rummy," Cecil said. The cars ahead began to crawl. He shifted gears and followed. The rain-sleek band of white concrete bent westward. He touched a signal switch and eased the van into the leftmost lane. He would use the Santa Monica Freeway on-ramp at La Cienega. "Dave, what do you want from me?"

Dave laughed bleakly, twisted out his cigarette, pushed the ashtray shut with a clack. "You'll brace anybody—truck bombers, homicidal maniacs, terrorists. But you haven't got the guts to tell one young girl the truth."

"It's not the same thing," Cecil said, "and you know it."

"And you know what I want from you," Dave said. "I want you to stop living a lie."

"I'm not living a stupid lie," Cecil shouted. "I'm not sleeping around. God knows, I'm not sleeping with you."

"God may not," Dave said, "but I sure as hell do."

"Yeah, well, that's how you wanted it. You made the rules. Only you're forgetting one today, aren't you? You weren't going to talk to me like this. It was none of your business. It was up to me to sort it out and do the honest thing, right?"

"Right. But I didn't know it would take you months." The blue velvet passenger seat was on a swivel. Dave turned it so as to face Cecil. "You know what I've begun to think sometimes, these nights alone? That I was wrong. When you came to find me, and said you wanted to stay, I thought this is nice but it can't last. He's young, he'll move on. But then I got to know you, and like a fool I let myself believe we had a bond between us nothing could break."

"We did." Tears ran down Cecil's face. "We do."

"Don't do that." Dave reached across and wiped away the tears with his fingers. "Nature decides. We like to think we can control it, but we can't." He swiveled the seat again, stared woodenly ahead. Past the moving wipers, cars crawled up the freeway on-ramp between banks of rain-washed ground ivy. "So, now it's Chrissie's turn. Lucky Chrissie." He forced a smile. "Well, you and I had four good years. When we get home, we'll drink to that. One last drink together."

"God damn you," Cecil said.

And no one said anything after that for a long while. Cecil jounced the van down into the yard of Dave's place from crooked, climbing Horseshoe Canyon Trail. Shrubs and trees here dripped onto uneven brick paving and made puddles. Dave's brown Jaguar stood by the long row of French doors that were the face of the front building. The storm had strewed the car with leaves and twigs.

It was noon, but the light here was dusky when they got down from the van, and Cecil dragged out of it Dave's grip and attaché case. Dave draped the trenchcoat over his shoulders again, and followed Cecil as he rounded the shingled end of the front building to a bricked courtyard shadowed by the gnarled branches of an old California oak. Cecil made a sound, stopped in his tracks, Dave blundered against him and banged a shin on the suitcase. He opened his mouth to ask, then didn't have to ask. He saw what Cecil saw.

A circular wooden bench hugged the thick trunk of the oak. On the bench stood potted plants. But a space had been left in case anyone wanted to sit on the bench. And a man was seated there. He leaned back against the tree trunk, head lolling to one side, hands open in his lap. The rain had soaked his hair and clothes, tweed jacket, wool slacks, good shoes.

"Is he asleep?" Cecil said.

"In this weather? If he is, he must be drunk." Dave went to the man, bent over him. His eyes were closed, but he wasn't asleep. He wasn't breathing. A pink stain was on his shirt, to the left of the breastbone. The rain had washed the bright red away, but it was a bloodstain. Dave laid fingers against the man's face. "He's dead."

"What's this?" Cecil bent and picked up something white and soggy and small from the wet bricks at the man's feet. A business card. He squinted at it in the gray light, gave a soft grunt, and passed the card to Dave. Dave dug reading glasses from a jacket pocket, put the glasses on, and read the printing on the card. He blinked surprise. "It's mine," he said, and put the reading glasses away.

"Who is he?" Cecil said.

"Beats me," Dave said. "Come on. He's sat here too long already." He moved toward a rear building, almost the same as the front ones, long and low. Both had been stables in some far gone past. The front one was now a rangy living room, the rear one had lofts for sleeping, a long couch in front of a big fireplace, Dave's desk and files. "He's cold as ice. Must have been here all night." He fitted a key into a door, pushed the door, and moved down the long room between knotty pine walls under naked pine rafters, to lift the receiver from the telephone on his desk. "At least all night. Maybe longer than that. Maybe days."

"Wouldn't the coyotes have found him?" Cecil laid the attaché case on the desk, and carried the grip up raw pine stairs to the north loft. "What do you think? Could they smell him in the rain?"

"They didn't." Dave sniffed his fingers. They smelled of the man's cologne. And tobacco. He lit a cigarette and waited, phone to his ear, to get through to Jefferson Leppard, Lieutenant, Homicide Division, LAPD. Leppard was a blunt-shaped, blunt-spoken young black with a passion for high-style clothes.

"Brandstetter?" he said. "I hope it's simple."

"I doubt it," Dave said. "I have a body for you."

"What kind of body?" Leppard said.

"The dead kind," Dave said. "Sitting in my patio."

"I meant, give me a description," Leppard said.

"Male, well-dressed, about thirty-five years old, fair hair, weight about one thirty, height about five eleven, a stab wound in the chest."

"You didn't touch it." Leppard sounded alarmed.

"I only touched his skin to check his temperature," Dave said. "He didn't have a temperature."

"Right," Leppard said. "This sounds like number six."

"I guess you'll have to explain that to me," Dave said.

Cecil came down the stairs at a loose-jointed run, sideways, two steps at a time. He lifted the coat from Dave's shoulders, took it to a standing rack by the bar under the north sleeping loft. He hung the coat up, and began to rattle bottles. Dave sat in the desk chair and told Leppard:

"I've been out of town. Up in Fresno for a week. On a case. Arson to cover murder. I just now got back. Cecil picked me up at the airport. What do you mean—number six?"

"We have a new crazy in town," Leppard said. "Serial killer. All stabbings, quick and clean and deadly."

"That's how this one looks—-very little blood."

"Victims all young males, in West LA and Hollywood mostly. Any reason for this one to end up at your place?"

"He had my business card," Dave said, "but I don't know him. He must have got the card from someone else."

"Are you gay?" Leppard said.

"I thought you'd never ask," Dave said.

Leppard laughed. "Sorry about that. But it's the connection. All the victims have been gay. We've checked them all out. Families, friends, fellow workers, lovers, bars, bathhouses, hospitals."

"Hospitals?" Dave said.

"That's the other connection," Leppard said. "That's why I was worried you might have touched the wound. It's blood that transmits the virus."

"Are you talking about AIDS?" Dave said.

"They all had it," Leppard said. "Every damned one."

"You coming to collect him?" Dave said.

"With my latex gloves," Leppard said, and hung up.

Cecil set a snifter on the desk. The brandy in it had a golden glow. Dave lifted the fragile bulb of glass and studied it. "Isn't this for after lunch?"

"I'm not staying for lunch. It's brandy because you said it's our last drink, and brandy was what we drank first, the night I blew in here four years ago. Never had brandy before. Remember that night? You got home late. I'd waited hours for you. Sat out there where that dead man is sitting now. In the night like him. Cold like him."

"Not cold like him," Dave said. "Cheers."

"Yeah," Cecil said glumly, "cheers."

And they drank together.

LEPPARD DRESSED SUBDUED today, to match the weather—eggshell brown oxford shirt, knitted tie and sweater in cinnamon, charcoal gray two-piece suit, Tuscan brown shoes. A clear plastic raincoat protected his clothes. They merited protection—he had a month's wages on his stocky body. A detective named Samuels arrived with him, a pale, fleshy youth in a fly-front coat. A lab man named Funt stepped around in puddles and snapped photographs of the dead man on the bench. Then he used a grubby little battery- powered vacuum cleaner on the dead man's clothes, scraped his shoe soles, clipped fingernails and hair.

Carlyle was the medical examiner. Dave had met him a number of times over the years. He had his helpers move the plants off the bench and do what they could to change the position of the body. Rigor mortis made the change grotesque. Dave turned away. So did Leppard. They walked out to the front, which was crowded by an unmarked police car, a black-and-white with a light strip on its roof, Carlyle's car, and a coroner's wagon. Two young uniformed officers sat in the black-and-white. Leppard leaned down and talked to them.

He looked at his gold Rolex, and walked back into the courtyard. Carlyle adjusted the clothes on the corpse and closed his kit. A bony man with gray skin and long teeth, he told Leppard, "Body's lost all heat." Rain beaded his glasses. He took them off and dried them on a handkerchief. "Stomach contents will tell me the time of death when I get him downtown. But it sure as hell won't be breakfast. He didn't arrive here this morning. He arrived in the night."

Funt's bulbous nose was red. He blew it on tissues and stuffed the tissues into a black raincoat pocket. He had a rubbery look, did Funt. His necktie knot was always crooked. "He didn't die here." Funt's voice was a wheeze. "There's grease, grit, old tire residue on him. He was stabbed in a garage, parking facility, maybe the street." He held up flakes of yellow in a plastic pouch. "Off his shoes."

"Some kind of flower?" Leppard said.

"Locust tree." Funt coughed. "At a guess."

Leppard grunted thanks, and now it was his turn with the body. He pulled a watch from a wrist, a chain from around the dead man's neck, rifled pockets for keys, coins, checkbook, wallet, an amber vial of pills. He opened the wallet and frowned. "No money. That's a switch. None of the other victims was robbed." Leppard passed a driver's license to Dave. Harold Andrew Dodge, born September 10, 1954. The photo showed a man thirty pounds heavier than this one but the same, no mistake. The address was in Rancho Vientos, formerly Fergus Oaks, now an expensive development. Dave gave the license back to Leppard, and put away his reading glasses. "I still don't know him."

"Ever heard the name?" Leppard tucked the license back into the wallet. "Still can't say how he came by your card?"

"Never heard the name," Dave said. "Still can't say."

The two men from the coroner's wagon were young, one Asian, one Latino. The Asian had skin like ivory. The Latino's face was scarred by acne. He was trying to grow a beard to cover the scars, but the hairs were sparse and silky. He said, "Lieutenant, can we have the body now?" A body bag hung folded over his arm. A collapsed gurney leaned against the leg of the Asian kid, raindrops twinkling on its chrome-plated frame.

When Leppard nodded his head, the Asian kid clicked and clacked the gurney open. The Latino boy laid the body bag on it and ran its zipper down. The Asian boy took the rigid shell of Harold Andrew Dodge in its rain-sodden clothes under its arms, the Latino lad took it under the bent knees, and they shifted it onto the gurney on its side, and worked the body bag over it and zipped the body bag. They wheeled the gurney away, rattling and tilting over the uneven bricks.

"What about Cecil?" Leppard said. "Does he know him?"

Dave said, "He doesn't know him." But was that a fact? *I'm not sleeping around.* Why had he said that? Dave had never suggested it. He trusted Cecil totally, as if a long life in a harsh business had taught him nothing. Cecil was startled to find Dodge's body here. But more startled than normal? Dave hadn't thought so. Yet he had cleared out fast after that drink. He had been in a tearing hurry to get away. Dave shook his head angrily to clear out the doubts. Leppard was manipulating him.

"He does live here with you." Leppard put watch, chain, the rest of the trove from the dead man's pockets into a five-by-eight manila envelope. He wrote on the envelope in ballpoint ink that the rain began to smear at once. He lifted the envelope to his mouth to lick the flap, then didn't lick it. Instead, he folded the flap and fastened it with the little metal prongs provided.

Dave said, "You're afraid of catching it."

"You damn right," Leppard said. "Aren't you?"

Dave felt cold in the pit of his stomach. Not for himself. For Cecil. Suppose that cry of denial had been false this morning. Suppose his shock at seeing Dodge sitting here had been deeper than he showed. Suppose Dodge had been Cecil's answer to a need Chrissie couldn't fulfill. And Dave wouldn't fulfill out of a stubborn sense of rectitude.

"It kills you in eighteen months," Leppard said. "But

that's not the worst." His expression was wooden. Dave knew a joke was coming. "The worst is, you lose all this weight. I couldn't wear any of my clothes. Hell, half of them aren't even paid for yet."

"Eighteen months makes killing them seem pointless," Dave said. "Who is this crazy with a knife?"

"Somebody who always hated queers. Like the religious nuts. All he needed was AIDS to set him off. I don't know. But eighteen months gets precious when it's all you've got. You said Cecil brought you home from LAX."

"But he doesn't live here anymore. He's got an apartment in Mar Vista. He married Christina Streeter, remember? The foreign correspondent's daughter?"

"Pretty blind girl," Leppard said. "Slipped my mind."

"Because it didn't fit your equation," Dave said.

Out in front, the heavy rear door of the coroner's wagon thudded shut. The side doors slammed. The starter whinnied, the engine rumbled, and in the damp noon quiet they could hear the tires crunch twigs as the black car rolled off down the canyon.

"What equation is that?" Leppard said.

"That I was homosexual, which meant Cecil was homosexual, and homosexuals don't marry. You don't want to think in accepted patterns, Lieutenant. Not in your job. Not about people in crises. I've been dealing with them for forty years. They seldom do what you expect."

Leppard looked at him but didn't answer. He drew breath. "The connection could be Juniper Serra hospital. The first five were all in there, one time or another. Maybe this one was, too. They get sick a lot. That's what the virus does."

"Right," Dave said. "Knocks out the immune system."

"So they go in for swollen lymph glands," Leppard said. "Or night sweats. Or diarrhea that won't stop." The rain began to come down hard. He winced up at it, hunched his shoulders, moved toward the cookshack at the side of the courtyard. Dave followed him. "Or sudden weight loss. Or weakness—can't stand on their legs to get dressed to go to work."

Dave opened the cookshack door for him, reached in and switched on lights, followed Leppard inside. Leppard unsnapped his raincoat. The stiff plastic rattled as he got out of it and hung it on a brass wall hook by the door. Dave closed the door, and began to look into cupboards.

Leppard said, "Or they get pneumonia. Or blue spots on the skin that turn into lesions."

"Kaposi's sarcoma." Dave brought sour rye bread from a cupboard. "Intestinal parasites. Brain parasites." He found butter, cheese, mayonnaise in a big refrigerator whose state-of-the-art works were disguised behind the oaken doors of a very old icebox. "I know they go in and out. Until they're too sick, too blind, or too crazy to go out again alive." He set the stuff from the refrigerator on the counter. "Sit down. A drink? They didn't go to any other hospitals?"

"Sure." Leppard drew out a pine chair at an old deal table scoured white, and sat down. "But Juniper Serra is a constant. I'm thinking of that male nurse a few years back, who killed all those dying old people."

"Not out in the street," Dave said. "Not in some parking garage, some driveway. In a hospital—with injections."

"Right." Leppard sighed. "Sure, a drink. Thank you."

Bottles stood in sleek ranks on a counter. Dave looked at them and raised his brows at Leppard. "Bourbon, please." Dave got glasses and ice. He poured Wild Turkey over ice cubes in a stocky Swedish glass for the lieutenant, and Glenlivet over ice cubes in a glass like it for himself. He took the bourbon to Leppard, who tasted it, opened his eyes wide, and said, "Now, that is something. Tell me, how do I go about becoming an insurance investigator?"

"What you want to ask"—Dave cut butter onto a grill—"is how do I get hold of thirty percent of the shares of a big insurance company. And the answer is, be the founder's only son—all right?"

"I'll start arranging that today," Leppard said. He drank lovingly again, and frowned. "If people act the opposite of what you expect, can you ever get so smart beforehand you know what the opposite is going to be?"

Dave shrugged. "Time and a long history of hit and miss help. And luck at the moment you need it." He busied himself stroking mayonnaise onto slices of bread. He rummaged out a bottle of Dijon mustard and smeared some of this on, too. He poked inside the refrigerator again, hefted out half a ham, cut thick slabs from this, laid these on the bread. He grated crumbly yellow cheese and piled this on the ham, closed the sandwiches, used a spatula to lay them in the sizzling butter on the grill. Now and only now, he shed the trenchcoat, hung it beside Leppard's coat, and brought his drink to the table. "Someone had a reason for bringing Dodge to me." He sat down opposite Leppard, lit a cigarette, tasted his Scotch. "It wasn't to threaten me. I don't know the man. I don't have AIDS. So it wasn't the killer who brought him."

"According to your theory"—Leppard reached across and drew a cigarette from Dave's pack on the tabletop, and used Dave's slim steel lighter to light the cigarette, and laid the lighter down again—"it was the opposite. Which means his mother brought him, right?"

"You'll have to ask her, won't you?" Dave said. "If she exists, you're the one who has to tell her that her son is dead. You have to do that, even if she already knows it."

Leppard shifted unhappily on his chair and sighed. Smoke blew out of his nostrils. He looked at the cigarette in his thick fingers. "You know, I haven't smoked in three months? See what this is doing to me? I hate that. I hate that part worst of all. Telling the family."

"Be blunt." Dave went back to the looming stove, took a look at the sandwiches, and turned them over with the spatula. His timing was right. The downsides were golden and crisp. The cheese was beginning to melt. "If you upset them, they may blurt things out they'd keep secret otherwise."

"I read the interrogation textbook," Leppard said.

"Forgive me," Dave said. He came back to the table for another swallow of Glenlivet, a pull at his cigarette. He didn't sit down this time. "I'm getting old. The old think nobody knows anything but them."

"I'll have to ask the mother if she knows you."

"Of course. But don't tell her I'm coming to see her."

"Maybe it won't be a mother. Sometimes it's a lover, a brother, a sister. Sometimes it's nobody. Everybody in their life deserts them. Like it was the plague. Leprosy."

"You didn't bring latex gloves." Dave returned to the big, hulking stove, all white enamel panels and nickel-plated trim, and eyed the sandwiches. "But the ME did. In the beginning, didn't the coroner's crews refuse to pick up AIDS bodies? Do we call this progress?"

"They threatened to fire them," Leppard said. "So, you going out to Rancho Vientos tomorrow? It's not your case."

"You going to stop me? He was sent to me. That makes it my case." Dave pulled plates down from a cupboard, laid the sandwiches on the plates. "This is rudimentary," he said, "but it should fill up the empty corners."

"Looks great." Leppard put out his cigarette, bent over the plate Dave set in front of him. "Smells great."

"I forgot napkins." Dave turned back for them, handed one to Leppard. They were yellow, to match the cupboards. He sat down, opened his napkin in his lap. "Why was he sent to me? Plenty of places to dig a shallow grave up here unseen."

Leppard shrugged, mouth full. He took his time, chewed, swallowed, drank a little more of his whisky. "You're famous. On Ted Koppel with professors, attorney generals. In *Time, Newsweek, U.S. News.* Any crazy could have picked you out."

"You're forgetting about the card," Dave said. "Do you remember Hunsinger?"

Leppard grinned. "You mean, speaking of crazies?"

"No." Dave bit into his sandwich. It was as good as he'd hoped. He wished it was Cecil sitting where Leppard sat.

"He's a psychologist. Looking after the street loonies, druggies, all the misfits, right? And writing books."

Leppard wiped his mouth, nodded. "Reams of paper."

"Well, he had a theory," Dave said, "that nobody does anything unaccountable, anything by mistake. Someplace in the back of the mind, there's a reason for everything we do."

"Like leaving a murdered stranger on your doorstep."

"Like that," Dave said. "I wish I knew the reason."

"So do I," Leppard said.

When Leppard left, Dave cleaned up the cookshack, switched off the light, closed the door, crossed through the rain to the rear building again. He lit the desk lamp, took ruled yellow pads out of the attaché case, set the case on the floor. He sat at the desk, lifted from a deep drawer a flat black case that held a little battery-powered typewriter. He zipped open the case, set the machine in front of him, rolled paper into it, stared at the blank sheet.

The big room was cold and damp. He went to the fireplace, slid back the screen. Kindling lay on crumpled newspapers in the iron basket. He set fire to the paper, placed a stringy-barked wedge of eucalyptus log on the sparking, snapping kindling, drew the screen across, went back to the desk. In Fresno, he hadn't used the yellow pads in order, so now he tore the scribbled sheets off, and shuffled them to get them straight. Glasses on his nose, he put fingers on the black keys with their white letters. For a moment. Then he gave a sharp sigh and picked up the telephone receiver. He punched the number of Cecil's workplace, the newsroom of Channel Three. In a minute, Cecil was on the line.

"Sorry to interrupt," Dave said, "but did you know Dodge?"

"Who's Dodge? The dead man? That his name?"

"Harold Andrew Dodge of Rancho Viento," Dave said. "You asked me if I knew him. Now I'm asking you."

"If I'd known him," Cecil said, "I'd have told you, Dave."

"That's what I thought," Dave said. "Just checking. Thanks." And he hung up and got to work, easy in his mind.

3

RANCHO VIENTOS LAY in a valley between low green hills. Big old oaks grew on the hills. The sea was not far off. Wind blew from the sea, strong, steady, with a salt tang to it, and today cold and damp. The sky was low, clouds in shades of ragged gray. This was still ranch country, cattle, horses, isolated barns in need of paint, in need of propping up. Here and there, a white clapboard farmhouse back from the road showed him fruit trees blossoming pink and white in door-yards, a goat or two, chickens pecking damp earth.

Beyond barbed wire, small herds of stocky, white-faced beef cattle browsed. A young palomino mare with a colt tagging her raced along beside a fence the length of the field, as Dave's Jaguar passed. Her taffy mane and tail blew in the wind. To his left, now, lay a sprawl of new, low, yellowish buildings on acres of freshly seeded, hardly sprouted grass. Oaks had been spared by the landscapers and they tempered the rawness of the buildings, walks, quads. A community college—that's what the roadside sign said it was.

He passed a new colonial style motel, the Oaktree Inn. And a mile farther along, the earth was torn up at a

17

construction site. Dump trucks stood around office trailers. So did big-barreled cement mixer trucks. But no one tramped around in the mud in boots and hard hats. No power saws whined. No hammers banged inside the raw concrete shells of what promised to be handsome buildings. No nails squealed from scaffolding being pulled down. Was it because of the rain no one was here? No. The answer was on a white enamel metal signboard in black lettering, on unpointed four-by-fours stuck in the ground. DREW DODGE ASSOCIATES, LAND & DEVELOPMENT. Everybody was in mourning.

Half a mile farther on, the highway turned into Main Street, a few blocks of old buildings, one story, two story, yellow brick, brown, red brick, chunky stucco, weathered frame. Hardware, seed and feed, auto parts, barber, farm machinery, Mexican, Chinese, all-American eateries, a movie theatre with a blank marquee. On a corner, a rickety three-story American Gothic hotel, brave with fresh white and green paint and polished bay windows with flowers sitting in them. A slumping red stone church. Where a new filling station stood shining across from a new two-story motel, Dave turned out of the main street, and made for the hills.

Here, handsome ranch houses sat on large lots behind white rail fences. Some were of used brick dry-brushed white or left in its own rough reds, with lots of sloppy mortar in between. Diamond-paned windows. Shake roofs. Shaggy old pepper trees, gnarled old olive trees, slim eucalyptus. Ivy geranium in the front yards, bougainvillea drooping off eaves. The roads curved with the curves of the hills, and driving the roads he glimpsed sometimes below him, shielded by high plank fences, grapestake fences, the blue of swimming pools in big backyards.

The house he wanted had a curved white gravel drive. The place was frame, bat and board, with the usual deep eaves. A big new American car, very dark blue, stood in the driveway. The garage doors, which faced the street, were down. He got out of the Jaguar and misty rain touched his face. The entryway to the house was deep, flower boxes on each side, marigolds, pansies. The entryway was flagged in shades of brown, yellow, red. The door was red with a brass knocker. It opened and a man came out. He carried a case. He was slight and for a moment in the poor light looked young to Dave. But he stepped from under the shelter of the roof edge into the sunlight and his hair was white and his face lined and there was loose flesh under his chin. He stopped in mid-stride when he saw Dave.

"No reporters, please," he said. "I'm Mrs. Dodge's doctor. She's exhausted. Didn't sleep all night." He looked past Dave in surprise. "No camera? No microphone?"

"I'm an insurance investigator," Dave said. "Have to ask her a few questions. It's just routine."

The doctor said, "The damned television news people are outrageous. There ought to be a law."

"There is," Dave said. "It's called the First Amendment. Were you his doctor, too? The family doctor?"

"Trowbridge," the doctor said, and held out his hand.

"Brandstetter," Dave said, and shook the hand. "Were you aware that he had AIDS?"

Trowbridge reddened. "Who told you that?"

"Foster Carlyle, the Medical Examiner in LA," Dave said. "He didn't tell me. He told the investigating officer, Lieutenant Jeff Leppard. Leppard told me. Last night."

"It's not the sort of information that needs to be spread," Trowbridge said. "No, I wasn't aware of it. He came to me last fall. He was losing weight. He was having night sweats." He squinted upward. "Going to rain again." He crunched across the gravel to his car. "It wasn't surprising to me. He's a workaholic. Puts himself under terrific stress. Never takes time for decent meals. I recommended a month's vacation—preferably out of reach of the telephone. Regular meals. Regular sleeping hours."

"And he never came back," Dave said.

The doctor opened the car door and put his case inside on the seat. He looked over the rooftop of the car, on which the sifting rain was spreading a shine. "No, he never did."

"You didn't know he'd been in Juniper Serra hospital," Dave said, "for pneumocystis carinii?"

"I've only seen the children," Trowbridge said. "It's impossible. That medical examiner must have mixed Drew's report up with someone else's. He couldn't have AIDS. He despised all of that—the drug culture, as they call it."

"Doctors are busy fellows," Dave said, "so maybe you haven't had time to read the statistics. Only seventeen percent of AIDS victims are intravenous drug users. Seventy-three percent are homosexuals."

"He was a family man," Trowbridge blustered. "Lovely wife, devoted to each other, two beautiful children."

Dave looked around at the handsome setting in its veil of rain. "Back in the real world," he said, "marriages last nine years with luck. Divorces are as common as weddings. Fifty percent of children are being raised by their mothers alone. Sex films come into your bedroom on television. On every street corner in LA boys run out to your car when you stop to sell you little envelopes of crack. Mom is a junkie, and the apple pie is laced with PCP. You lead a sheltered life out here, doctor. You're out of touch."

"Drew was no homosexual—he loved sports, for heaven's sake, racquetball, jogging, the gym. Before he got caught up in this shopping mall project of his." Trowbridge grimaced. "Then there was no time for anything but work."

"Contaminated blood?" Dave said. "From a transfusion? Any transfusions in the last seven years you remember?"

Trowbridge shook his head. "No accidents. No surgery. No transfusions. No."

Dave gave him a thin smile. "We seem to be narrowing the options, don't we? You never suspected? He never came to you with a venereal disease? Herpes, hepatitis? No rectal injuries? Nothing that would suggest to you—?"

"Absolutely not." Trowbridge acted fretful. "He was under a lot of stress, lately. Maybe he saw"—the frail shoulders moved uncomfortably—"some, some, some woman. Prostitutes spread AIDS."

"That would be nicer, wouldn't it?" Dave said.

Trowbridge glared. "I'm due at the hospital. But I'm going to phone that medical examiner. He's made a mistake."

"Then so did whoever killed Dodge," Dave said. "We have a serial murderer in LA these days. Five young men stabbed to death in the same way as Dodge. All of them AIDS victims. All homosexuals."

"You didn't know Drew." Trowbridge glanced up grumpily at the rain. "He was the most open, sunny, natural, outspoken young fellow in the world. It's fantastic to suggest he had some dark, sordid sex life no one knew about."

"Someone knew," Dave said.

"Well, don't upset Katherine." Trowbridge put a leg into his car. "Don't tell her."

"I expect she already knows," Dave said. "She'll have had a phone call from the health authorities by now."

"Then she kept it from me. She wouldn't do that." Trowbridge dropped into the big car, slammed the door, started the engine. Dave rapped on the glass of the passenger-side window. With a grimace of annoyance, the doctor touched the button to lower the window. "You'll have to tell her, if she doesn't know," Dave said. "And if they were the loving couple you think they were, you'll also have to treat her. You'll also have to watch her die." Trowbridge glared at him and angrily rolled the window up again. He drove the dark blue car away over the crackling gravel of the drive, out past the white rail fence, down the curving street. Dave turned, took steps over the flagstones, lifted and let fall the polished brass knocker on the red door.

He had time to glance twice at his watch before the door opened.

A short woman in her fifties stood there, in a fresh blue warm-up suit, new jogging shoes, a dish towel in square freckled hands. She was stocky, gray-haired, wholesome-looking. "I'm Gerda Nilson. What do you want?"

Dave told her his name, took from a pocket the ostrich-hide folder that held his private investigator's license, let it fall open for her to read. "I need to ask Mrs. Dodge a few questions. I won't keep her long."

"Can't you read the police report?" the woman said. "That black man—Lieutenant Leppard from Los Angeles—he asked a hundred questions. Yesterday. It took hours. I thought he'd never leave. In my time, Negroes—"

"Came to the back door," Dave said.

Her blue eyes narrowed, she tilted her head. "Brandstetter? He mentioned you. It's not an easy name to say, but it's hard to forget."

"He said Drew Dodge's body was found at my house, right?"

"Yes." She frowned. "So, you're not investigating for somebody who hired you, like on TV?"

"Nobody hired me," Dave said. "I'm investigating on my own. I never saw Drew Dodge in my life till yesterday. Am I right—you're a member of his family?"

"His mother-in-law," she said.

"Did he ever mention me? He had my business card. I didn't give it to him. Do you know who did? Or why?"

"Why he'd need a private investigator?" Her mouth twitched grimly at a corner, she stepped out to him, and pulled the door shut back of her. She lowered her voice. "Lately, he'd run into bad trouble. I don't know the particulars, but it must have had to do with the mall. It was worrying him before he went to the hospital, but this last week, I'd say things had got really bad." She stood tiptoe to reach Dave's ear. "I think he was scared to death."

"I passed the construction site on my way into town," Dave said. "It looks like quite a project."

"Oh, millions of dollars," she said. "Why, it's going to change the whole lifestyle of this valley. Sears-Roebuck, fashion shops, an enormous supermarket, anything you can name." She remembered, and the sparkle went out of her eyes, the years showed up in her face. "Was. I don't know, now." She regarded him in the gray rainy light. "No, he never spoke your name. And I don't know what he'd need with your services. Except that he wasn't himself after he came back from the hospital. He was depressed and jumpy. Not himself at all."

"Because of his health?" Dave said.

"Oh, no. That was fine. He'd lost all this weight, and now he felt so much better, and he was going to gain it back, and, oh, no, he was real cheerful about that. No, it was something else. Trouble with the shopping mall. What else could it be?"

"He didn't talk to you about his business problems?"

"He wouldn't worry me." She shook her head decisively. "He wouldn't worry Katherine or the children. He was cheerful and sunny all the time—no matter how hard he worked, sometimes all night long. It was his nature." Her lower lip trembled. She bit it. Tears showed in her eyes. "He was the dearest boy. The dearest boy." She used the dish towel to wipe away the tears. "Come in. It's cold out here." She opened the door, motioned Dave inside ahead of her, hung his coat in a crowded closet. In the entryway, two spider bikes, one red, one blue, leaned between two six-foot-tall ficus trees in tubs. Stairs led down to a long, beam-ceilinged living room with an inglenook fireplace and furniture that looked comfortable and jumped-on. Videotape boxes were strewn on the wall-to-wall carpet in front of a big console television set.

Dave said, "Do you live here, Mrs. Nilson?"

"I live in Minneapolis," she said, "but I come out for Thanksgiving and stay through till the snow melts back there. Mr. Nilson died five years ago, and I'll admit it—I get lonesome. But I think they like having me. I try to pay my way, cooking, looking after the youngsters. That lets Drew and Kathy have some time together." She gave a short laugh. "It did, until this shopping mall thing took over Drew's life. Then I was company for Kathy, wasn't I?" She tried for a smile. "Sit down. I'll get us some hot coffee." She moved off with a laugh. "It's not sunny California today."

"I wonder if you can let me have a picture of Drew?"

"A picture?" She turned. "Oh, no. He was deathly afraid of cameras. There's not a picture of him in the house. So easygoing he was about most everything. But no pictures. Not on your life. We had to laugh about it."

"Can you tell Mrs. Dodge I'd like to see her?"

"I'll take her some coffee, too." She paused in a far doorway. "Dr. Trowbridge gave her something to make her sleep, but maybe coffee will keep it from working right away. I'll try."

"Thank you," Dave said.

And she came, barefoot in jeans and a bulky sweater, looking pale and drawn, dark circles under her eyes, eyes red, maybe from fatigue, maybe from weeping, maybe both. She was her mother's daughter, no mistake. Same snub nose, same slightly uptilted blue eyes. But slim and trim. Among those cassettes must be Jane Fonda's workout tapes. Fragile Kathy Dodge did not look. Strong enough to drag her husband's body from dark Horseshoe Canyon Trail into Dave's courtyard in the rain, and prop it on that bench? The dead man hadn't been heavy. Dave watched her drop disconsolately onto a couch and set the coffee mug that matched Dave's and her mother's on a table piled with architecture and interior design magazines, investment magazines, kids' magazines. Dave said:

"I'll be quick about this. I know you're tired."

"I'm more than tired," she said. "I wish I were dead."

"My name is Dave Brandstetter," he said. "Did Drew ever mention my name to you?"

"No." She eyed him dully, shook her head. "Never."

Dave pulled a typed paper from inside his jacket, unfolded it, put on his reading glasses. "Did he ever mention any of these people to you? Bill Bumbry? Art Lopez? Sean O'Reilly? Frank Prohaska? Edward Vorse?"

She rubbed her forehead, sat wearily forward, picked up the coffee mug. "I don't know." She drank. "I don't think so. I don't remember. I'm sorry. I'm just—too damn tired."

"Try, Kathy," her mother said. "Mr. Brandstetter's had a shock, too. It was in his patio where they found Drew."

"What?" The young woman jerked her head up, both hands pushing at her hair. "Found Drew? Where?"

"It's all right." Dave folded the paper, pushed it away, sat forward, made to stand up. "I won't keep you anymore."

But she held up a hand. "No, wait." She frowned at the pocket where the paper had disappeared. "Let me see."

He pulled the list out and gave it to her. She frowned over it for a moment, then passed it back. "I think Art Lopez worked for him. At the construction site. He died."

"The same way as Drew." Dave pushed the paper away and rose. "Thank you." He turned to the mother. "Thank you, Mrs. Nilson." He walked toward the steps up to the entry way, stopped there, turned back. "One last thing. Did he seem frightened to you lately?"

"He had terrible nightmares," Katherine Dodge said. "He'd wake up screaming. But he wouldn't tell me why."

"I'm sorry for your loss," Dave said.

He got his coat and went out into the rain again.

4

HEADING FOR THE construction site, he changed his mind on Main Street when he saw lettering on windows above a corner hardware store. The building was narrow brick, 1887 on its cornerstone. The ground-floor windows were large and framed in wood many times painted white. On the panes of the upstairs windows was lettered DREW DODGE ASSOCIATES.

It was no trouble to find a parking space. Few cars lined Main Street. In the square across the way, rain dripped from seesaws and swings under big, dark, weeping trees. He pushed coins into a parking meter, turned up his collar, and looked for the door. It was down a side street, thick glass, DDA lettered on it. It wasn't locked. He climbed a narrow, walled-in staircase. Under its thick new carpeting, old treads creaked. There was a smell of paint.

At the top, instead of the narrow, dim hallways and brown office doors that must have been here once, he found a cheerful, open reception room under a ceiling of lighted panels. There were planters, bookshelves with clusters of pottery. Handsome chairs and couches. No one sat at the reception desk where a telephone burred and blinked small lights. A Rolodex sat next to it. He dug out reading glasses and standing, knees bent, riffled through the little cards. But he found no names that meant anything to him.

"Anybody here?" He put the glasses away.

The drawer of a file cabinet rolled closed somewhere, and a woman came from behind a partition. She wore a tight-waisted blousy sort of jumpsuit in a shiny black cotton fabric, with a wide belt that had a gold buckle. Her eyeglasses were very big, with round lenses tinted amber toward the tops. A heavy gold chain circled her throat. She was as trim and slim as Katherine Dodge but fifteen years older. Her throat was stringy. She brushed dust off her hands, whose nails were long and painted to match her amber glasses and the amber tint of her fluffy hair. She crouched and unplugged the telephone cord at the wall, stood again, smiled.

"How can I help you?" she said.

He gave his name, showed his license, said he didn't want to interrupt but had a few questions. Who was she?

"Judith Ober," she said. "I manage the office. Did."

He shook her hand and put one of his cards into it. "Have you seen one of these before? Did Drew Dodge ever mention my name to you—or in your hearing?"

She frowned at the card, looked up. "No. Why?"

"Because when I found his body on my doorstep the other day, a card like that was on the bricks between his feet. Where did he get it? He was a stranger to me."

"Your doorstep? I didn't know. How awful for you."

"But you did know he was killed. Yet you're working. Why is that? They're not working at the construction site."

"I'm not working. I came to get my belongings. I have a future, Mr. Brandstetter, but it isn't in Rancho Vientos. Drew Dodge Associates was Drew Dodge—period. All by his clever, charming, handsome, devious self. Without him"—she lifted and let fall her hands—"all this will vanish."

"Where will you go?" Dave said.

"North. Silicon Valley, I think. Don't worry about me. I'm a treasure, and that's the kind of money I make." She laughed briefly, sadly. "I can't get out of it now. It's far too late. They printed statistics lately on us career gals over thirty-five. Nobody is going to marry us. I kissed the boys goodbye after college. I knew what I wanted. And I got it. And I loved it. And now I'm stuck with it. Forever. Which makes you think. Somebody ought to write a self-help book—*Never Make Decisions When You're Young*."

"If you don't," Dave said, "someone will make them for you. That's no good either. Will you get severance pay?"

"Surely you jest," she said. "I haven't been paid in weeks. Cash flow. You know cash flow? Well, around Drew Dodge Associates, cash stopped flowing some time ago."

"Then it's not out of respect for the boss's memory that the construction workers aren't out here today. It's because they haven't been paid."

"And he's not around to con them into believing they'll get their checks any day now. He could do that." Her smile was mournful. "He was a charmer-and-a-half, that boy." Dave frowned. "The shopping mall won't be finished?"

She shrugged. "All I know is it's going to take money. And money there is not."

"What happened to it?" Dave said.

"Cost overruns and leasing shortfalls—a deadly combination. Most of Drew's investors were small-time— doctors, dentists, lawyers, professors at the local state college, businessmen, shopkeepers, people who want to see the valley grow. Bud Hollywell, our Senator in Sacramento. Pete McCaffrey, who owns the local paper. Drew kept close to Pete."

"Because he could influence opinion?"

"Why, Mr. Brandstetter"—she batted her eyelashes— "what a thing to say. Haven't you ever heard of friendship for friendship's sake?"

"What you're saying is that there weren't enough big investors, and the small ones had run out of money?"

"They'd given till it hurt, most of them. A good many their entire life savings. Drew was persuasive."

"Maybe they were having second thoughts," Dave said. "His mother-in-law says he was worried. About the mall."

"He had three hundred thousand in materials and labor to pay off in the next ninety days. That would worry most of us. It's the obvious guess, isn't it? But I was closer to Drew than his mother-in-law. Gerda? As innocent as they come. You can't help loving her, but Minneapolis is never going to turn anybody into a sophisticate."

"'The dearest boy,'" she called him," Dave said. "Wasn't he the dearest boy?"

"Among other things," Judith Ober said. "But it wasn't like him to let money get him down. Money wasn't that important. He never had any trouble in his life getting money when he had to. He started with nothing, you know, and made himself a millionaire by age thirty." She picked up a handbag. "You want a drink? Lunch? There's a tiny place at the end of a little shopping arcade up the street that fixes divine crêpes."

In Rancho Vientos? Dave didn't believe it, but he wanted a drink, so he let her lead him there. The room was small, with blonde tables and woodwork, fake Tiffany lamps, a corner bar stocked with good liquor. And she was right about the crêpes. He had sweetbreads, she had shrimp. She drank a martini from a glass the size of a birdbath. Dave drank Glenlivet. It was quiet. No other customers came. The rain whispered on a skylight above hanging plants.

"A man like Drew Dodge," she said, "doesn't let sensitivity to others slow him down. He made his start by selling the house the Nilsons had given Katherine and him for a wedding present. With the profits, he began buying up places seized by the State for delinquent taxes."

"Was that what killed Mr. Nilson?" Dave said.

"Funny you should mention him. You look a lot like him. No, John thought Drew was smart as paint. Rags to riches in five years? What a son-in-law!" She worked on the martini, took tiny bites of the crêpe. "Drew got into land qua land after that. Bigger and bigger parcels. At first, he sold to developers. Then he thought, why let them make all the money, and he opened this place and became a developer himself. Not with his own money. With anybody's he could get his hands on. He was good at that. As you say, 'The dearest boy.'" She twitched a wry smile. "Not that he ever lied to anybody—not intentionally. He talked himself into believing what he was selling, and then turned around and sold his fantasies as if they were rock-solid truth."

"And always figured he could do it one more time?"

"And he could, too. If he hadn't gotten sick." Her bright toughness went slack for a second. She was angry and gloomy. "That's what did it. Those weeks in Juniper Serra with that terrible pneumonia. You should have seen what it did to him. He tried to keep going here, but he wasted away. He was so weak. Finally we had to send for an ambulance."

"And he lost his grip on the shopping mall project?" Dave said. "You couldn't have carried the responsibilities for him? You said you were a treasure."

"He never told me enough," she said grimly. "But even if I'd known it all, it needed him, his personality, his plausibility, his optimism. I don't know." She sighed, shook her head, drank deeply from her big glass again. "It's too bad, damn it. I'd love to have seen him pull it off. He was feeling well again, scared of something, but not the shopping mall thing. He'd have found a way. And then some LA crazy stabs him and puts an end to it all."

A youth who didn't look like a waiter but who wore a starchy white coat came and clumsily took away their plates. A ranch hand was what he looked like, nose sunburned, back of his neck sunburned. Or maybe a pumper of gasoline and changer of spark plugs at a highway filling station. He brought the desserts—ice cream in goblets with Grand Marnier poured over it. He carried the glasses with great care, as if he'd only encountered such fragile items for the first time today.

"The end to it was coming anyway," Dave told Judith Ober after the man went back to the kitchen. "He had AIDS." She frowned, spoon still midway to her mouth. She set the spoon down with a rattle in the saucer under the goblet. She took her glasses off. "You're not serious."

Dave nodded. "You never suspected he was gay?"

She blinked thoughtfully. "He had that boyish charm. But this is a man's town, Mr. Brandstetter. And he was very much the man among men. No. It never crossed my mind to think he was gay. What a con man."

"Was he conning his family about his long hours? All those nights he worked on through, never went home?"

"Did he tell them that?" She smiled wryly. "It's not in character. If he couldn't turn work into play, he didn't do it. He breakfasted with investors, played tennis, racquetball, golf with potential lessees, took contractors to dinner at expensive restaurants, threw parties for them all every weekend at his home. He met with his accountant once a month, his lawyer every three months. Opened his own mail, made his own phone calls. His voice was beautiful. I'll miss it."

"Opened his own mail? But didn't you type the answers?"

Her mouth twitched. "To the letters he let me see."

"Where was he, then, those nights he didn't go home?"

"His mileage vouchers say far away," she said. "His banks, S and Ls, restaurants, bars, golf courses, all his contacts, business, social, were in this area. Yet he drove hundreds of miles each week. Where to—Los Angeles?"

"If you want to lead a double life," Dave said, "the big city is the place to go, and Los Angeles is closest."

She picked up her spoon, tried the ice cream, remembered something. "Do you know what? He used to keep a leather jacket in his closet at the office—the kind with chains, you know, sort of Hell's Angels-ish? And boots, those low ones with straps and buckles. Motorcycle boots. Good God." She laughed at herself. "Cliché of clichés, and I didn't add it up at all." She smote her forehead with the heel of a hand. "And I called Gerda Nilson naive."

"The jacket and boots," Dave said. "They aren't there now?"

"I haven't seen them in months."

"Do you remember a construction worker named Art Lopez?"

She didn't answer for a minute. She looked into Dave's face, blinked, put the glasses back on. Mechanically, she took another spoonful of ice cream. Then she said, "Oh, boy," and laid the spoon down. "Yes, I remember Art Lopez. And shall I tell you why? Because of all the people involved out at the construction site, half a dozen different contractors and their foremen and their crews—the only one I ever saw more than once or twice in the office was Art Lopez. And he was a hard hat, that's all. Riveter, welder? Something." She fluttered a hand. "And not much more than a kid. Small, but good-looking. He took to coming to the office to see Drew about the time I was set to go out to lunch."

Dave said, "Was he still there when you got back?"

"Sometimes," she said. "So that was how it was?"

"You tell me," Dave said. "What became of Lopez?"

"He got sick and quit. Then someone said he died." Dave told her how Art Lopez died.

"I guess I don't want to eat this." She pushed the glass away. "What are you saying? That it was Art who gave Drew AIDS?"

Dave shrugged. "Maybe. Maybe the other way around. It can stay in the system years before it surfaces, you know. With Dodge, it surfaced as pneumocystis carinii. Which meant he had thirty-five weeks to live." Dave looked around for the sunburned youth, saw him, raised a hand, called, "Coffee, please?" Dave looked at Judith Ober again. She had lost color. He said, "Don't worry. Office managers can't catch it from washing the boss's coffee mug."

She touched her face. "He used to kiss me on the cheek."

"Or from being kissed on the cheek," Dave said.

"How do you know so much?" she said crossly.

"I'm a great reader," Dave said. The gas pump jockey came with their coffee. When he'd gone, Dave said, "Have you got a complete list of personnel at your office? I could ask the LAPD for it, but they don't want me interfering with their case."

"Ask them for what?" she said dully.

"Art Lopez's address," he said.

She picked up her cup, blew at her coffee. She nodded, but absently. She was worrying behind those glasses. Not with her common sense. With primal panic. Thinking she was too young to die. From a coffee mug, from a kiss on the cheek. Thinking it was a hell of a note.

5

IT WAS THREE in the afternoon, and still raining. Art Lopez had lived on a side street of look-alike apartments near Hollywood Boulevard and Western. The buildings were beige stucco boxes propped on tall steel pipes, living quarters above, parking below. The structures turned square blind faces to the street. Stairs climbed to galleries along the side, where doors and windows showed. Stairs and galleries were beige, too, with railings of frail wrought iron. Potted begonias sat here and there, drooping in the rain. They gave a touch of color, but the main effect of the street was one of dreary tidiness.

Dave left the Jaguar under a big tree that was dropping powdery yellow blossoms into the gutter. These trees lined both sides of the street. He looked at them thoughtfully, remembered Funt, leaned on the wet hood of the Jaguar, and bent a knee so as to see the sole of his shoe. Yellow blossoms were mashed onto it. He was in luck. He noted a pair of bulky motorcycles under blue tarps on greasy, gritty cement in one of the garage spaces. He climbed stairs, walked the gallery, looking for a door numbered nine. It was the last door. He pushed its bell button. Except for the gentle patter of the rain, the neighborhood was quiet. No one came, and he worked the bell button again, keeping his thumb on it. Radio music stopped inside. And after thirty seconds, the door opened. A young woman stood there in a terrycloth bathrobe, drying her hair with a blue bath towel. She was brown-skinned, not fat but sturdy, in her early twenties. Her hair was black and cut boy-short. Her soft brown eyes opened wide. She knew who he was and she was surprised as hell to see him. But she didn't say so. She said: "Who are you? What do you want?"

"Art Lopez used to live here. Did you know him?" Dave held out his license in its folder. "Can you tell me anything about him?" He tucked the folder away.

The brown eyes studied him. A pink tongue moistened a well-shaped mouth. She looked away for a moment, glanced quickly at Dave, and turned back into the apartment, scrubbing her hair once more. "Come in," she said. Dave stepped in and closed the door. The place smelled faintly of ammonia. It was not a feminine place. It was nothing in particular. Beige walls, beige carpet, matching couch and chairs in tough yellow-and-brown-striped fabric. A small television set on a cart. A plain blonde coffee table. She went down the room, crossed a little hallway, sat down in a bathroom to comb and blow-dry her hair. Over the whine of the dryer, she called, "Art lived with me after he got AIDS. He was my brother, and my mother and father threw him out."

"He gave this address at work." Dave shed his coat. "I thought he quit work when he got sick." Dave sat down.

"He didn't quit till he couldn't hold his welding torch no more. He kept sending them money from his pay, even when they treated him how they did."

Piled on the coffee table were dog-eared magazines, *Time, Newsweek, U.S. News,* others, next to a gray mound of newspaper clippings. He shuffled through them. The subject was always the same. AIDS. He had a file drawer filled with identical grim reading matter up in the canyon. Labeled, dated, tucked in manila envelopes. The news kept changing.

"How did it come," he called, "that Art was well enough to go out and get stabbed in the street?"

"With AIDS you get remissions sometimes. The doctors—they can patch you up, make you feel better. For a while. He was going blind. Chorioretinitis. You know about that?"

"CMV," Dave said. "Ordinarily harmless."

"If you got AIDS," she called, "nothing is harmless." The whine of the drier stopped. She moved out of the bathroom, to her left. She called, "He didn't feel great, but he wanted to see everything while he still had time, you know? I took him around, Disneyland, Magic Mountain, Universal Studios Tour." She came out of the hallway, dressed in pudgy fresh jeans, a fresh blue sweatshirt. "What the hell. He looked after me when we were little. He took me around. A girl, a pest, a baby, but he was always good to me."

"He was alone when he was stabbed," Dave said.

"I work from four to midnight." She went into a little kitchen of wood-grain plastic cabinets. "At a hospice for AIDS victims. When I seen what was happening to Art, I got some training. Everybody don't want to do it, you know. They are scared. They don't believe you can only get it from having sex or sharing needles. Hospital workers don't get it. A little Clorox bleach will clean up the worst mess you can think of." Pottery rattled. "It's my wake-up time. I made coffee. Will you have coffee? Or a beer? I kept beer here for Art."

"That's fine," Dave said. "Why did he go out alone?"

"He was gay. From about fifteen, he liked to cruise. I think he got to remembering that, missing it. Got lonesome for the parks, the bars, the streets."

"He was sick, dying," Dave said. "Didn't he care that he'd give his sickness to others, that they'd die, too?"

"He cared." A refrigerator door sucked open and slapped shut. "Did I say he went out for sex? He was too weak for that. He just went out to visit the old places at night, where he'd had good times, okay?"

"Maybe," Dave said. "What's your name?"

"Carmen." She came and put a cold can of beer into his hand. "One good thing. He never knew what hit him in that alley. He couldn't hardly see nothing at night no more." She returned to the kitchenette. "The police, that black cop, asked me all this. Wasted hours. Why? Why aren't they out catching this maniac?" She came back with a coffee mug, stood holding it, blowing at it, watching Dave through the steam. "And you? Why have you come?"

"You know why." Dave tasted the beer. It was very bad. "A sixth man has been murdered in the same way as your brother and the others. Someone left his body at my house for me to find. I didn't know the man. So why was he brought to me? I live in Horseshoe Canyon, he lived in Rancho Vientos, a long way off. I drove out there this morning. And I was told this man knew your brother. That's why I've come. To find out about Drew Dodge."

She blinked, but her round, smooth brown face showed no expression. She drank some of her coffee. "I never heard of him," she said.

"Art never mentioned him?" Dave said. "He and Dodge were lovers. Wouldn't he have told you that?"

"You don't listen," she said. "He cruised. He didn't have lovers. All he wanted was one-night stands."

"I think Dodge came to see your brother."

"If you got AIDS, nobody comes to see you. Nobody came."

"How would you know? You said you work at night."

Her young face settled into hardness. "Why would he come all that way? Not for sex. Art was dying, here." She turned sharply away, banged refrigerator and microwave doors. "I am one who is trying to help, to make the pain a little less for these suffering ones. Would I murder them?"

"No one's accusing you," Dave said.

"Then why come here about this Dodge?"

"He was here," Dave said. "They found yellow blossoms from the trees out front here on his shoes."

"Those trees grow all over LA," she said. "If you want to get involved—" She leaned on a counter that divided kitchenette from living room. Small potted vines sat there, salsa bottles, cardboard salt and pepper shakers, a stack of paper napkins. "Go find the one who stabbed my brother to death. The police will do nothing. What do they care? He was only a faggot. Worse than that, he had a disgusting disease from doing disgusting things with his sex. They are happy Art is dead. They wish all faggots were dead." A microwave timer dinged, and she turned away. "I have to eat now, and get to work."

"I'll go." Dave set the beer down, pushed to his feet. "If I can just make a quick trip to the bathroom?"

"*Sí*." Her back was turned. "Help yourself."

He glanced at her as he passed. She stood eating small supermarket burritos off a blue pottery plate. In the little hall, he closed the bathroom door smartly, then stepped through a door at right angles to the bathroom door. Into a bedroom. Clothes were strewn around, the same sort she was wearing today. The door of a closet stood open. Sweaters and jeans, a handful of simple dresses, cotton prints mostly, blouses. Her raincoat, teal blue. He rummaged. At the end of the rack, he found a leather jacket, well-worn. In the rainy light from a window, he made out flaking painted initials on the back. AL. Then his hands touched more leather. This jacket he pulled off its hanger and held up to look at. It was newer than the other, heavier, more expensive, a larger size. No initials on this one. Of course not.

"What are you doing in here?" Carmen stood in the door.

"This was Drew Dodge's." Dave dropped the jacket on the bed, bent into the closet, came up with a pair of heavy, low-top boots. "So were these. He came here, Carmen. He came here night before last. The night he was murdered."

"You can't prove it." Her eyes were scared.

"Before that"—Dave set the boots back in the closet—"he hadn't been here for five or six weeks, had he?"

"Why do you want to make trouble for me?" she said.

"You managed that all by yourself," Dave said. "He'd been in the hospital, very sick. He was only just back on his feet, only just able to drive again."

Her laugh was harsh. "Why would he come here? Art is dead—remember?"

"You're his sister. You sheltered Art, looked after him. That cost you. You don't bring home big paychecks from that hospice, do you? Drew Dodge was well off. Why didn't he come to bring you money? And to talk about Art? He had a wife and children, he had straight friends. But nobody he could talk to about Art. Nobody but you."

She looked paler. She pressed her mouth tight, so her lips lost their nice shape. She worked her lips tightly together, as if trying to keep the words inside. At last, she said softly, "*Sí*. All right." She nodded. "He did come here. He was good and kind. He did bring us money. To pay the rent. He brought the microwave, to make cooking easier for me when Art was sick."

"And night before last?" Dave said.

She shivered, hugged herself, turned away to face the window. "It's cold, isn't it, this rain? I wish the rain would stop." She turned, brushed past him, reached into the closet, and lifted down the raincoat. She flapped into it, cinched the belt at her chunky waist. "He tried to come."

"Tried?" Dave said.

"He parked on the street. His car is still over there." She was dull-eyed now, spoke tonelessly. "He crossed the street. But he didn't make it up the stairs. He died, down below, stabbed, like Art. When I got home from the hospice, I found his body in my parking space. Beside Art's and his Kawasakis." She smiled bleakly. "Drew bought those. They were not very good riders. They just drove them to the bars, you know? Those bars where they make believe they are tough *hombres*, all right? Biker bars, leather bars. Only, of course, it is all fantasy." Her laugh was mournful.

"And it was you who brought him to my house," Dave said. "That was a mistake, Carmen. A very bad mistake. You should have called the police." She didn't answer. She looked stubborn. Dave asked, "Why did you pick me?"

"Because you are smart and you figure out stuff when the cops can't. I seen you on television. We all did, one night last fall. A discussion show. And Drew said you were gay. Somebody told him. Art bet you were not."

"Art lost," Dave said.

"Everything," she said bitterly. "But I forgot about you till I found Drew's body, and your card was in his hand. And I thought, somebody has to stop this. The cops don't care. They will never do nothing. Maybe you would care. Maybe you would stop it. I put him in my car and drove to Laurel Canyon. It was hard to find your place in the dark. How did you know it was me? I thought no one would ever know." She gave him a sheepish smile. "I forgot how smart everybody says you are. I was shook to find you at my door."

"I got lucky," Dave said. "Where did he get my card?"

"He couldn't tell me, could he?" she said. "I never meant to leave it there. I just dropped it." She half reached out to him. "You won't tell the cops?"

"They'll want to see the place where he was killed," Dave said. "They may find a clue that will lead them to the one who's doing this."

Her mouth turned down scornfully. "They will not. They will arrest me."

"No. They were killed at night. You work at night."

"They will arrest me for moving the body, then they will lock me up and make me prove I was not the killer. You must not let them do that. I am needed at the hospice. There's not enough of us now. People quit. It gets to them."

"If you want me to track down this killer," Dave said, "I have to keep my license. If I conceal what you've told me, I'll lose it."

"I see." She sat down heavily on the edge of the bed. It wasn't made up yet. It showed sheets bought at a bargain someplace, different patterns for the upper and lower, different patterns still for the pillow slips. All florals, faded from many washings. She said, "Well, I'm not sick, not dying. So I can't complain, can I, no matter what? But the blows keep falling." She smiled up at him, bravery in the smile, but no happiness. "I lost Anita, I lost Art, and because I would not let him die cold and starving in the streets, I lost my mother and father, too. AIDS was God's punishment on Art, and because I took him in, God has damned me, too, right, and they don't speak to me no more." Her laugh was sad. "But that would have happened, anyway. They are going to guess the truth at last—that I'm gay, too." She raised her eyes to Dave's again. "That I will never give them grandchildren. That the girl I shared this apartment with was my lover."

"Was?" Dave said. "What happened to her?"

"When Art came, he was very weak. We had to carry him up the stairs. He had an accident. Diarrhea. He couldn't help it. Then he told us he had AIDS, and Anita took her stuff and split. I mean, while I was cleaning him up in the bathroom, twenty minutes. She didn't even say goodbye. She ran. I went to see her where she works, where we used to work together, and she wouldn't come out of the factory yard. I had to talk to her through the fence. She stood way back, afraid I'd breathe on her. I tried to give her stuff to read, so she'd see there was no danger to her. She wouldn't take it. We loved each other a lot. But she was too scared."

"I'm sorry," Dave said. "Tell me—do you think Art knew somebody was out to kill him?"

"He didn't say nothing like that." She shook her head. "He wouldn't have gone out, would he?" Her shoulders sagged. "I wish he was here. It gets very lonesome. I miss Anita."

Dave touched her hair. "Where's your phone?"

She stood up quickly. "You aren't going to call the cops?"

"Abe Greenglass," Dave said. "My lawyer. We'll want him here first. Then the cops. There's no way around it, Carmen."

"But you will stay, too?" Her eyes pleaded.

"If you want me to," Dave said.

6

SOMEONE HAD TURNED on the ground lights, a thing he often forgot to do. The rain sparkled in the lights, danced on the old brick paving of the yard. Amanda—it was her car that stood in the place usually filled by Cecil's van. She had been out of touch for a time. Or he had. He smiled at the notion of finding her here. He hated coming home to an empty place. He was growing tired of it, growing tired of living alone, growing tired, to be honest about it, of living. It was why he kept taking on jobs not worth his time. To kill the time. To keep busy. He swung the heavy Jaguar in beside the little, cloth-topped Bugatti.

The windows of the cookshack glowed a cheerful yellow through the rain. He ran across the courtyard, splashing through puddles, and bolted into wonderful, welcome warmth and cooking smells. Amanda was small and neatly put together, her hair a dark, shiny helmet. She laughed, as he hung up his coat. "There you are. I was afraid I'd have to eat all this myself." He went and kissed the top of her head, dragged out a chair at the table, sat and pulled off his shoes. She said, "Where have you been?"

"Downtown, Hall of Justice, helping keep a young woman out of jail. What's to drink?"

"You tell me." She wore a red wraparound apron. The color brought out a rosy flush in her cheeks. She was very young. Still. His father's ninth wife and final widow. Carl Brandstetter had died racing his Bentley along a midnight freeway—how many years ago now, six, seven? He'd had a heart attack, not his first. It had taken Dave a long time to get used to his death, but at last he'd settled for the idea that the old boy would have wanted it that way, sudden, no hospitals, no hanging on, no turning into a feeble wreck of himself. He'd been a big, bluff, handsome Viking of a man, with an outsize appetite for life and all the best things in life, including a hefty share of those that were far from free. Amanda had loved him—it was hard not to love him—and had missed him when he died. She'd wandered around the huge rooms of that Beverly Hills mansion desolate for weeks, until Dave took her in hand, and set her to remodeling this place for him. From that, she'd gone on to other jobs for friends and strangers, then set up shop on Rodeo Drive and prospered.

She said, "I decided it's bourbon weather, but I couldn't decide if that meant a Manhattan or an Old-Fashioned."

"How about a Manhattan in a tall glass," Dave said.

"Ah, a Sundowner," she said, and went to sorting through the double stand of bottles on the counter. "And exactly who is this young woman, and why would anyone want to put her in jail?"

"She moved the body of a murdered man," Dave said, watching Amanda locate a thick, squat Swedish crystal pitcher, take a fistful of ice cubes from the big oak refrigerator, and measure Old Crow and sweet vermouth over the ice. She was carefree with the booze, letting it brim over the top of the jigger. She licked her fingers appreciatively before she reclosed the bottles. She uncapped a little paper-wrapped bottle of Angostura bitters, shook drops from this into the mixture in the pitcher, then began turning the ice in the pitcher slowly round and round with a glass rod. "There's been a series of stabbings," Dave said.

"The police haven't found the killer yet. One of the victims was Art Lopez, this young woman's brother. A homosexual. An AIDS victim. Like all the others." Amanda turned and stared at him. "Carmen wants the killing to stop. This one took place in her garage. The dead man was a friend of Art's. And hers. He had my business card in his hand. She knew a few things about me. She thought since the police weren't getting anywhere, I ought to try. She brought him here and left him for me to find. Out there. On the bench under the oak."

"Good Lord," Amanda whispered. She turned soberly away, reached glasses down from a cupboard, put ice into these, poured the glowing deep-red mixture from the pitcher over the ice. She set the pitcher in the refrigerator, and took the glasses to the table. After she'd set them down, she drew out a chair and sat herself down. "And are you going to try? It all sounds hideous."

"The police have dozens of men on the case," Dave said. "I doubt that one more would make a difference. Carmen's not too clear in her thinking. You can't blame her." Dave tasted the drink, grinned, lifted the glass to her. "Just right," he said, set the glass down, lit a cigarette, frowned. "She figured because I'm homosexual I'd work harder and get more results than the LAPD. Her idea is that cops despise gays and don't care that they're being slaughtered—especially gays sick with AIDS."

"Is she right?" Amanda tried her own drink.

Dave shrugged. "About common police attitudes—yes. That they don't want to catch the killer—no."

"So you're not going to help." Amanda was disappointed.

"I've already done that. I went out to Drew Dodge's bailiwick and found a connection between him and Art Lopez, and found the place where Dodge was killed, and telephoned the police. They found his BMW parked on the street, matted with yellow blossoms brought down from the trees by the rain. They found a neighbor who saw a tall, skinny stranger hanging around about midnight, a street kid in rags, long blond hair, a bandana for a headband. I helped. What's wrong?"

She was staring. "Did you say Drew Dodge?"

Dave nodded. "A young, slick-talking developer in Rancho Vientos. Wife, kids, showy house, country club, all the conventional trappings of success. Who used to have quickie sex with one of his construction worker hard hats in the office at noon. Art Lopez, right? And spend the nights on motorcycles, visiting the gay bars with him in LA."

"And he had AIDS, too?" Amanda asked softly.

Dave said, "Did you know him? Don't tell me you knew him."

"I'd met him." She nodded slowly, troubled. "Radiant. A real charmer. What a shame." She shivered, and her look at Dave was mournful. "Met him at a party at Madge's, last autumn. He was building a shopping mall. Tom Owens was there. He was the architect. Madge was to do the wallpapers for the boutiques, the fabrics for the offices— working with Lloyd Noonan. Lloyd designed the interiors."

"Small world," Dave said. "Did Dodge tell you he was in trouble and needed the services of a private investigator? Did you give him my card?"

"I never saw anyone who looked less troubled in my life. He was sitting on top of the world. He simply glowed."

"Maybe Madge gave it to him." Dave stretched an arm up to bring down from the end of a cabinet the receiver of a yellow telephone. He punched a familiar number. Madge Dunstan was one of his oldest friends. They went back to the 1940s, just after Dave had returned from the rubble of Germany, where he'd been a very young intelligence officer, trying to sort the Nazis from the good guys after the war. Dave had been introduced to Madge in the dark-paneled, leather-padded little bar of Max Romano's restaurant by Rod Fleming, a novice interior decorator Dave had set up house with. Rod was twenty years dead now, but Madge was vitally alive, working better than ever. The phone rang in the vast white rooms of her seaside house, but no one picked it up. He pressed the cutoff button. Maybe Tom Owens had given Dodge that card. Years ago, Dave had saved the architect from death. They'd been friends ever since. Not seeing a lot of each other, but friends. He punched Owens's number. He, too, lived at the beach, in a place he had designed in the dunes, that looked a little like the wreckage of a ship, all prows and planks. No one answered at Tom Owen's, either. He sighed and hung the receiver up. Amanda had gone to the stove.

"Drink your drink," she said. "Supper's almost ready."

"It's kind of you to do this." Dave worked on the drink, put out his cigarette, lit another. "But I'm puzzled. You haven't been around since New Year's. You realize that?"

She bent, opened the oven door. Heat rushed out. Dave felt it. She used big quilted mitts to lift a casserole out and set it on a counter. She closed the oven door. "I realize that. I've missed you. I've just been terribly, terribly busy. The oil millionaires are leaving Beverly Hills, going home to Abu Dhabi and all those romantic places, to their camels, their endless cups of syrupy coffee. The yuppies are moving in. No deep carpets for them, no velvets, no cushions, no purple and maroon and gilt. They want nouvelle interiors, all sleek and white and bare and bright. And Amanda Brandstetter aims to please."

"And in the midst of all this," Dave said, "pity for the loneliness of her elderly son-in-law transforms her for a night into a happy little homebody?"

She lifted down plates from a cupboard. "You got it."

"I don't think so. What do you want?"

She turned and blinked hard at him, her face more flushed than before, and not just from the heat of the oven. "You're terrible, do you know that? What a way to talk." She turned away again, and pulled a spatula from a drawer. "Do you know how rude that sounds?"

"I guess it does." He put out the cigarette. The smell of the tobacco was interfering with the glorious aromas drifting to him from the casserole. "I'm sorry about that. I'm glad to see you, regardless. Okay?" He heard a familiar noise through the wash of the rain on roof and bricks outside. He got up and went to the cookshack door and pulled it open. He stood there in the cold, damp air, waiting, while behind him Amanda made sounds, laying the table with mats and flatware and glasses. Cecil came into Dave's line of sight, lit by the outdoor spots under the eaves of the long buildings. He came jumping puddles, shoulders hunched, jacket pulled up to cover his head. Dave pushed open the screen door for him. He wiped his feet in long Nikes on the sisal mat outside, and came in, laughing.

"Is this the right ship?" he said. "It doesn't look big enough for all those animals lined up out there." He peeled off the windbreaker and hung it up. Dave closed the door, shut out the cold, the rain, the sound of the rain. He looked at Cecil, who ambled over to Amanda to give her a kiss. He looked at Amanda.

"It's a plot," he said. "I knew it."

"That must be what it means to be a detective," she said.

"Ho-ho." He went back to the table. Cecil joined him there, holding plates on which lasagna steamed. It was a recipe Dave had wangled out of Max Romano decades ago—the best lasagna in the world. Cecil set a plate at Dave's place, another at Amanda's. Before Dave could reach it, he snatched the wine bottle and took a corkscrew to it. "My favorite food. My favorite people." Dave peered at the label of the bottle in Cecil's hands. "A wine straight from the wedding at Cana. Don't tell me it's not a plot."

"Sit down." Amanda brought a third plate to the table, laid it at Cecil's place. He squeaked the cork out of the bottle. She shed her apron, hung it up. Playing cellarer, Cecil splashed an inch of wine into Dave's glass for him to taste. Going along with the foolishness, Dave tilted up the glass, rolled the wine on his tongue, swallowed, nodded. Cecil grinned and filled all their glasses. He set the bottle down in the middle of the table, and pulled up his chair. Amanda laid a napkin in her lap. "It's a plot," she said. "Eat."

Dave looked hard at Cecil. "The animals lined up two by two. Where's your mate? Where's Chrissie? Doesn't she get any supper?"

"At the marina," Cecil said. "With Dan'l Chapman and his folks." He laughed briefly and shook his head. "Little old Dan'l is still crazy about Chrissie. He really hates my guts. When I dropped her off, he was there to meet us at the condominium gates, you know? I thought he was going to punch me out right then."

"There's a thought," Dave said. "Maybe he and I between us could beat you up. Childhood and old age."

"Dave, will you stop that old age nonsense," Amanda said sharply. "I never knew anyone younger in my life."

"Chrissie and Dan'l talk on the phone every day. Hours. She says he's lifting weights at a gym." Cecil crowded his words with food, chewed for a moment, swallowed, drank some wine, set the glass down with a click. "He'll be able to take me on alone—in two or three years. He isn't exactly bulging with muscles yet."

"You're dodging the point." Dave tasted the lasagna. "Why are you here, the two of you, and not Chrissie?" The food was flavorless. Not because Amanda didn't know how to follow a recipe. If Max Romano had cooked it himself, Dave wouldn't have enjoyed it. Not tonight. "You want to move back. And not alone. You want to bring Chrissie with you. You want to hop from one sleeping loft to the other, right? You think Chrissie is so blind she wouldn't catch on?"

"Dave, stop," Amanda said.

Cecil sat staring down into his plate. He waited for a moment. Then he said quietly, "She likes you and she misses you. You know how much overtime I put in. She needs more company than that. She's alone in the dark, Dave, all the time. I'm not enough."

Dave drank some wine, took another mouthful of the food he didn't want. "She and I would be company for each other—is that what you're saying? You really screwed up, didn't you? You wanted her to be happy. You want me to be happy. But neither of us is happy. And you're miserable." A tinny car door slammed out on the trail. Frowning, he got to his feet. "Straighten it out, young Harris. Tell her why you did what you did, apologize to her, and—"

The lights went out. In the kitchen and outside. Dave tumbled his chair over backward. He moved through darkness as deep as that Chrissie lived in, groped for the door, found the knob, pulled the door open, pushed open the screen. Amanda said something behind him, but he didn't catch the words. He stepped out onto the wet bricks before he remembered his shoes. He'd taken them off. At his shoulder, Cecil said: "It's the circuit breaker. I'll go."

"No." Dave caught his arm and dragged him back. Very roughly. "You stay here, look after Amanda. It's probably an outage, a line down. A tree. Rain loosens the roots and they fall. But if it isn't, then I think I know what it is. And I'm sore as hell at you, but I don't want you killed."

"I don't want you killed." Cecil jerked from his grip.

"Stay here, damn it," Dave said, and ran into the dark, stumbling, the uneven bricks bruising his feet. He ran toward the looming silhouette of the front building. The power box was at the far front corner of that building, where the lines could reach it handily from the trail. There was a streetlamp that hung high among leafy branches where Horseshoe crossed Sagebrush Road. A little light from that far corner reached here, but not much. He reached the front of the building where his car stood, Amanda's runabout, Cecil's van, all of them glinting faintly with rain.

He ran between Amanda's car and the French windows that fronted the building. And somebody jumped out at him. He flung himself to the side, felt the fender of the Bugatti bang his thigh, felt a searing pain along his shoulder. He saw a ghostly glimmer of blond hair, saw a skinny arm raised, the flash of a steel blade. He dropped to the bricks, and rolled under the car. Cecil shouted. A gun went off. Dave knew the sound. It was the SIG Sauer nine-millimeter semiautomatic he kept in a drawer on the loft of the rear building. Cecil had more presence of mind than he did. Fast footsteps fled over the bricks, splashing rain. The SIG Sauer went off again. Close by. Out on the trail, the tinny car door slammed, a rackety motor revved and clattered off downhill.

"Shit," Cecil said. "Dave? Where are you?"

"Give me a minute." Dave made to crawl out from under the car, and the pain from his shoulder was so bad he fainted. He woke to find Cecil on hands and knees, peering at him, eye-whites, a glint of teeth.

"Are you okay?"

"He cut me, but I'll live," Dave said. "Switch the lights back on, will you?"

"Damn." Cecil scrambled to his feet and went off to the power box. Dave heard Amanda's quick steps in the wet. She sounded breathless. "What's happened? Dave? Cecil?"

"Call an ambulance," Cecil said. "He's bleeding."

The lights came on. And Dave saw that Cecil was right. He lay in a puddle the wrong color for rain.

7

DAVE HADN'T HEARD the rain stop. He had slept deeply, darkly, drugged by painkillers an emergency room nurse had shot him full of at a hospital where they'd sewed up the slash in his shoulder. Samuels from the LAPD had looked wan in the glare of the white room. Leppard was off duty and couldn't be located. Samuels, in his fly-front coat, pointed a pocket tape recorder at Dave, while Dave sat on a steel table with his shirt off, being repaired. Every time the doctor made a move, Samuel winced as if he was the one wounded. The puffy hand holding the recorder trembled.

"Did you get a look at his face?"

"It was too dark. Maybe it wasn't a him. It could have been a her."

"Jesus," Samuels said. "You think so?"

"I think it was the tall skinny street kid your witness saw hanging around Carmen Lopez's apartment building before Drew Dodge was killed. Long blond hair. Headband."

"Girls aren't generally tall."

"Not generally." Dave nodded. "Forget I said it could have been a her. It's a habit I have—never taking anything for granted." He forced a smile. "All right?"

"No, you got a point there," Samuels said. "The car?"

"Old, an American economy model from the late sixties or early seventies. Dark. I don't know the color."

"License number?" Samuels said hopefully.

"Sorry." Dave shook his head. The dope was taking hold of his brain. "The time was 7:10 P.M. He pulled the main switch on the power box and knew I'd come to see what was the matter, and he waited and jumped me in the dark." Dave looked past Samuels's pale bulk at solemn Cecil and anxious Amanda waiting for him beyond the half-glass doors of the emergency room. "My friends came out of the house and scared him off."

"You see the knife?"

"Not to be able to identify it," Dave said.

Samuels squinted uncertainly at the small metallic box in his hand, found what he appeared to hope was the correct button, and switched off the recorder. To bandage Dave's shoulder, the doctor shifted position. Samuels peered around him at Dave, forehead wrinkled. "What do you think? Was this our serial killer?"

"Dodge was robbed," Dave said. "None of the others was robbed. I'm not young. I don't have AIDS."

"Yeah, right." Samuels sounded discouraged. He said thanks, said he'd be in touch, dropped the tape recorder into a pocket of his pale coat, and pushed out of the room. He threaded his way between a crowd of hurting men, women, children waiting with faces dulled by pain, standing, sitting on molded plastic chairs, lying on the floor, eyes closed.

The doctor's name was Patel. He was small, spare, brown-skinned, with large, luminous dark eyes, long lashes, and a grave demeanor. In his elegant Karachi accent, he insisted Dave stay in the hospital overnight, in case infection developed, fever, who knew what complications. He had already arranged for a room for Dave. But Dave wanted to go home. He was dogged about it. He was fine. There'd been no nerve damage. The sewn-up cut would mend. He wanted to sleep in his own bed, on his own loft, under the skylight. In the end, not liking it, Patel gave him pills and let him go.

Cecil had dropped him and Amanda back at the house on Horseshoe Canyon Trail, then gone on to pick up Chrissie at the marina, and take her home with him to their Mar Vista place. Amanda had stayed, had slept in the guest room on the loft, watchfully, getting up to look at Dave from time to time. The boards of the loft had loud creaks built into them, but he hadn't heard her. He'd stayed under in his dreamless darkness until noon. Then she'd fixed them breakfast in the cookshack. Like Dr. Patel, she'd argued hard against his leaving his bed.

"I'll bring your breakfast on a tray."

He pushed clumsily to a sitting position, swung his feet to the floor. "No need for that. But I'll need help dressing, if you don't mind."

"You're going out? Dave, no way."

"Have to go out." He tottered to his feet, pulled open the pine doors of a wardrobe. "Dig back in here for me, will you, please?"

She dug and brought out shabby, secondhand clothes he'd bought at thrift shops. "What in the world are these?"

"Camouflage," Dave said.

"You're not going to shave?" she said.

"More camouflage." It was clumsy getting into the clothes but they managed it between them. He pushed his feet into stained and ragged tennis shoes. "Sorry. Can you tie these for me?" His arm was in a sling. She knelt and helped him.

"Why camouflage?" she said.

He smiled and stood up. "The game is afoot, Watson."

"Oh, please," she said. "Don't joke. Look at you. You're white with pain."

"That's hunger," he said.

After breakfast she demanded he let her drive him wherever it was he simply had to go. He'd used up precious energy talking her out of it. He sat in the Jaguar now, thankful for a minute to rest. The ride the machine gave him was gentle, but the painkillers were wearing off and the slightest motion made his shoulder hurt. He had to let the pain come back. He couldn't drive drugged.

Kevin Nakamura owned a service station down the canyon at a main cross street. The station was yellow flagstone and glass, and sheltered by slim eucalyptus trees. Nakamura, in starchy suntans, was using a wide, stiff-bristled push broom to sweep leaves, twigs, seedpods into the sun-dazzled street. He was a tidy young man. Neatness mattered to him. He concentrated, and did a thorough job. One of the help could be doing it, but the help were working under cars in the shop, and filing receipts in the office among shiny stacks of motor oil cans. And their sweeping wouldn't have satisfied Nakamura. He kept his head down, and got every last twig, leaf, pod.

Dave tapped the horn. Nakamura came to the car. Dave wore a moth-eaten ski cap.

Nakamura said, "You want the old car."

"Will it start?" Dave said. "Is there gas in it?"

"I keep it ready for you," Nakamura said. "That was our agreement, right?" He grinned with large, white teeth. When he did that, his eyes almost closed. He shook his head. "You look like a real bum."

"Flattery will get you nowhere," Dave said and, moving carefully, got out of the Jaguar. At the moment he did that, the sun stopped shining. He looked up. Black, ragged clouds were scudding in from the southeast. It was going to rain again. He watched Nakamura walk off bowlegged to the rear of the station building. In a moment, he came back into view, driving a pale yellow sixties Valiant with a deep crease along one side, where it had got the worst of a sideswipe collision someplace in its past. It was as tinny as the car driven last night by the kid who had attacked him. On another case, years ago, Dave had driven the Jaguar into a neighborhood of street gangs and nearly had it stripped. He wasn't going to repeat that mistake. He handed Nakamura the keys to the Jaguar. "Don't let anything happen to it."

"I'll tune it up," Nakamura said. "When will you be back?"

"Before you close," Dave said. He winced, wangling his long lean limbs into the small car. The seat was tattered under him. Getting a grip on the door to close it was awkward. Nakamura saw that, and closed it for him. He leaned at the window, worried.

"What happened to your arm?"

"Somebody tried to remove it," Dave said.

"You sure you're all right to drive?"

"No," Dave said. "But it's too far to walk."

It was Chandler Park. And not as he remembered it. He remembered it from his teen years. A gospel temple with a big white dome loomed above the trees north of the park. For a few months in high school, Dave had yearned over a handsome classmate who adored Lizzie Tremaine, the flashy evangelist who had built the temple and presided noisily over its meetings in flowing white robes and brassy yellow hair. And Dave had tagged down here after the boy for a few Sundays, just to be near him. It was useless. Jesus was the only male that boy would ever love.

But it was then that Dave had come to know this place at the heart of LA. Brick apartments from the 1920s along one side, hulking old three-story frame houses with jigsaw-work porches and bay windows on the other two sides. The neighborhood hadn't been exactly upscale even then. In the decades since, paint had peeled, window screens had rusted out, glass had been smashed and replaced by cardboard, or nailed over with plywood. The brick buildings had fared a little better, but not much. Shops were mostly deserted, doorways piled with blown trash. The lettering on painted signs faded over the doors of Mexican cafés. A corner grocery looked flyblown. A place that claimed to sell records and tapes had padlocked grillwork over its doors and windows, and no one inside. Still, life went on upstairs.

He heard voices when he parked the car and got out into a misting thin rainfall. Human voices, television voices. Music from boom boxes, very loud. The television voices spoke Spanish. The other voices spoke black. The music was black. A clutch of black teenage boys slouched at the far corner. Across from them, Latino boys slouched also, watching them. In the park, a solemn, white-haired, heavyset Mexican in plastic rowed a boat on the lake among ducks. He hinged the oars inside the boat, and rummaged in a white plastic supermarket bag, and began tossing bread to the ducks. A young pregnant black woman passed Dave as he fed the parking meter. She was pushing a pram with a baby in it. The baby was looking up at the rain, blinking, giggling. An old white woman bundled in many layers of coats and sweaters and stockings shuffled past. She was bent with the weight of four shopping bags. A man whose color no one could tell crept on hands and knees out of an alleyway and called to Dave. The man was hanging on to a bottle in a paper sack. Dave knew he was being stared at, so he swore at the man and went on.

He found the doorway he wanted. The number was right. It stood half open on a narrow stairway that stank of urine and years of greasy meals. Beer cans, fried chicken boxes, cigarette butts strewed the stairs. A bulging, green plastic garbage bag leaked stinking wetness where it had been dropped and forgotten. Light was supposed to come into the hallway of the second story, from windows at either end, but the windows were grimy and the light outdoors was poor anyway. He looked up. In sockets along a smoky ceiling the splintery fragments of light bulbs showed. The walls were dense with spray-painted names and curses. He went along the hall, trying to read numbers on doors. Then he climbed to the third floor, and located the number, and knocked. Loudly, because the hall was filled with all those mingled noises.

A shout came from the other side of the door. He wasn't sure of the words. He tried the knob. Locked. He sensed he was being watched. He stepped to the stairwell. Below, a plump man in a fly-front coat moved quickly out of sight. Samuels? Dave ran down the stairs. Nobody. He climbed back to the door, rapped again. "Who that? What you want?"

"Bill Bumbry," Dave said.

"He don't live here no more. He passed away."

"Did you know him? Can you tell me about him?"

Locks clicked, the door opened a crack, a face peered out, a black, bony face, bloodshot eyes. At Dave's belt level. "Was you a friend of Billy's? One of the gay ones?"

"Did he have any others?" Dave said.

The man smiled faintly. "Not white, he didn't."

"I'm trying to find out who killed him." Dave took out his license and showed it at the narrow opening. "I'm a private investigator. Can I come in? It's noisy out here."

"And smelly." The man shut the door, rattled the chain loose, opened the door. He sat in a wheelchair, in an old brown flannel bathrobe, a grubby blanket covering legs that ended at the knees. He let Dave step past him, and closed the door, whose spring lock clicked. "I don't believe God would ever send a black person to hell. We got it here. Every day of our lives." Chuckling, toothless, he rolled his wheelchair backward. This was easy: the room was almost empty. A narrow bed, beside it a little table with a lamp, a clock radio, a Bible. On the floor a television set with a cracked shell and bent rabbit ears. A doorless cupboard in a corner, shelves lined with cans of Dinty Moore beef stew. On the counter a hot plate and three charred saucepans. A grimy refrigerator, a sink with dishes in it. A door half open on a dark bathroom where the toilet box ran and ran.

"I can't be too hospitable," the man said, and tilted his head slightly, to indicate he meant the state of the room. "You can sit on the bed if you want. It's pretty clean. I change it every week."

"Thank you." Dave sat on the bed. His shoulder hurt. "What happened to your arm?" the man asked.

"Somebody attacked me with a knife in the dark last night," Dave said. "I wondered if it might be the same one that killed Bill. I came to find out if anyone ever saw Bill in the company of a skinny blond kid with long hair. Maybe a teenager. Keeps the hair back by folding a bandana and tying it around for a headband."

"Not me," the man said. He held out his hand. "I'm Dixon." The knuckles were swollen, gnarly. Dave shook the hand gently. "Billy's uncle. I haven't lived here long. He lived here with his daddy, my brother. I saw Billy sometimes. He had his troubles, being so, well, like a girl? From a little child, you know—it made things hard for him with the other children. Poked fun at him, hit him. Lost his mama early, too. That made it worse. His daddy tried to beat it out of him. Mason would never hit Dandy—that his dog. Just the boy. And I was the one Billy run to. I let him cry to me, I was kind to him. Why not? Wasn't his fault. God made a mistake, is all—put a girl in a boy's body."

"But he lived with his father?" Dave said.

"Right here. I'd have had him with me, but I'm crippled. Railroad accident. No way I could look after a child. No money. Railroad lawyers seen to that. Disability all I get, and that ain't scarcely enough for one, let alone two."

"He grew up," Dave said. "Why did he stay?"

Dixon shook his head. "Don't make sense, do it? But he did. And he earned the money. Short-order cook. Suited Mason fine, laying around all day, free food and lodging, all the six-packs he could drink. Never changed how he treated Billy—same ugly mouth. But Billy looked after him. And the dog. See that wallpaper? Billy's hand. He loved things to be pretty."

"I think he knew who killed him, all of them did. The medical examiner couldn't find any sign they'd put up a struggle before they were knifed. You never met his friends?"

"Police asked me that, too," Dixon said. "He never brought nobody when he come to see me." The wrinkles in his forehead deepened. "Could you call them friends, that kind?"

"Did he mention any names?" Dave said. "Did he know any of the other young men killed the same way—Art Lopez, Sean O'Reilly, Frank Prohaska, Edward Vorse, Drew Dodge?"

Dixon listened hard, frowning, but he shook his head. "No, I heard those names on the TV news, but not from Billy."

"Why isn't his father living here now?" Dave said.

"Scared of infection. Billy got AIDS, you know. And Mason, he took Dandy and moved out. Took all the nice furniture Billy bought, too. Left Billy here on a mattress on the floor, sick by himself. Claimed to me he was feeding him. You know what that meant? He got hamburgers in bags, and he sent Dandy up the stairs with them. "Go take it to Billy," he'd say, standing down there in the street door. Well, Dandy, he just a dog, and when he got up the stairs out of Mason's sight, he ate the food. He never brought it up here, never."

"Wonderful," Dave said.

"But they good folks in this building, some of 'em. And one come and told me Billy was alone and sick and starving, and I used a pay phone and called around County offices I know, and one of 'em sent help, got him into a hospital. I paid the back rent here and moved in to hold the place for him. And after a while, he got strong enough to come back. I didn't know him, he was so wasted. And then he went out the other night, and somebody killed him with a knife."

"He never said he was afraid that would happen?"

Dixon shook his head. "All he was afraid of was AIDS."

8

He followed patchy traffic up Alvarado through the rain. There was an odd tightness in his throat. Cold sweat covered him. He wanted the rattly car to get him home. It had been a mistake to come out. He would hit the bed and sleep. Or maybe he wouldn't make the effort to climb to the loft. He'd just pass out on the couch. It had been a long time since he'd felt this bad. Motorcycles stood bunched at a curb in front of a shabby stucco building with a sign in faint, sputtery red neon tubing, THE MOTO-CROSS. It had the look of a place used only after dark, but a youth in chain-hung leather, boots, greasy dark curls, came out the door, carrying a crash helmet. He winced at the daylight, paused to put on the helmet, then straddled one of the motorcycles.

Dave turned off Alvarado and found a side street of hulking frame houses that had quartered USC students in the past. Very old, thick-trunked date palms lined the curbs. So did cars, sad specimens mostly, wheels to get to work on. Now and then a ten-year-old Lincoln or Cadillac had a shine to it other than what the rain put there. Bought cheap, when the price of gas went high. At last Dave found a place to park the Valiant, then trudged back through the sifting rain to the bar. He only pushed the door half open, only got half a blast of the rock music from inside, the roar of voices, jeering, laughing, howling, when a big hand was placed flat on his chest, and he was pushed back outside. A bearded young man followed the hand. He stood six foot five and weighed three hundred pounds. "Private meeting," he said. "No visitors."

"I'm an insurance investigator," Dave said. "Yearly inspection." He dug out his folder and flashed his license. "And I can tell you, I've got a lot to look for. The County doesn't like gay bars anymore. Any excuse they can find, structural, wiring, hygiene, food handling, ventilation, too many customers for the room, anything, they'll close you down, here. I can help you avoid that."

"You don't look like no insurance man," the giant said. He breathed out beer fumes. "You look like a wino."

"I didn't want to scare the customers," Dave said.

"Shit." The giant looked up and down the street, as if an answer would come from there. But no one was on the sidewalk. It lay dismal in the rain, littered with soggy hamburger wrappers, pizza boxes, Coke cups. "Today? This is a business meeting, man. Come back tomorrow."

"Tomorrow I'm busy." Dave tried to step around him.

"Shall I break your other arm?" Goliath placed himself between David and the door. "Give you a matching pair?"

"The County thinks gay bars spread AIDS," Dave said.

"Bullshit. You don't get AIDS from drinking Coors."

"Right. But I seem to remember a few years ago, on an afternoon like this when the place was closed to outsiders, a team of police kicked in that door, and found a naked boy chained facedown to the pool table. Everybody in the place had a go at him."

"It was a frame-up," the giant scoffed. "We should have known. It was the kid's idea. He asked for it."

"Maybe," Dave said, "but it's a way to get AIDS in a bar."

"Chrissake, I know that," the man said. "We cleaned up our act now. We collect toys for crippled children."

"Uh-huh. Did you know Art Lopez? Early twenties, short, good-looking, a construction welder? He used to come here."

Ajax shrugged. "Anybody can come here."

"With his lover, a blond man in his mid-thirties. They wore jackets and boots like yours. Crash helmets. They rode twin motorcycles. Kawasakis."

The giant scowled. "He was killed. By the knifer in the dark. Couple weeks ago. The other one got it the same way, when, last night, night before last? They both had AIDS."

"They came here together, didn't they?" Dave said.

"You're no insurance man," Hercules said. "You're a cop. You're on that case. Yeah, they used to come here—last fall. So what?" He snorted. "You should have seen them ride those bikes. Like a couple of Sunday school teachers. They didn't kid nobody except theirself."

"Who did they party with?" Dave said.

"Nobody," the big man said. "Each other."

"Never a tall, skinny kid in ragged jeans, long blond hair, a bandana headband?"

"Is that who they think done it?"

"It's who tried to do it to me last night," Dave said.

"Shit." Fafnir took a backward step, alarm in his eyes. "You got AIDS, too? Ain't you a little old for it?"

"A little," Dave said. "No, I ain't got AIDS, too. But I seem to be frightening somebody. I wondered if, since two of the victims haunted this place, their killer did. If he chose his victims here."

"No tall skinny kid in ragged jeans," the big man said. "It's leather or nothing here. We don't serve you if you don't come dressed right. Anyway"—again he looked along the rain-gray street—"it's the wrong neighborhood. The killings were all in Hollywood and West LA. Pansyville."

"It's not that far away," Dave said.

"It's another fucking world," the giant said.

"The skinny kid may be a false lead," Dave said. "Do you own a knife?"

Samson growled, clutched Dave's jacket, sweater, shirt in a fist, lifted him off his feet, thrust his whisker-matted face into Dave's. "Listen up. It wasn't me, okay?" He set Dave down, glowering at him. "I'm not into violence."

"I'm happy to hear it." Dave smoothed his old clothes.

And from nowhere came Samuels in his fly-front coat and tan hat, holding up a snub-nosed detective special, and panting. "Everything all right here?" he said to Dave, and to the big man, "Police officer."

"No problem, sir." The giant showed his teeth and took another step backward, hands raised. "Little misunderstanding, is all. Bar's closed today."

"For Saturnalia," Dave said. "A few months late, but who's counting?" Samuels blinked his pale eyes. "Saturn what?"

"Monthly business meeting," Atlas said.

"We seem to be running on parallel tracks," Dave told Samuels. "If I buy you lunch, will you drive me home?"

"You don't look like you feel so good," Samuels said.

"That is the understatement of the week," Dave said.

They had moved him. This was a different room. That was all he knew. Not even whether it was day or night. He seemed to see the rainy rectangle of a window sometimes, sometimes the glare of fluorescents. Once a keen little beam of light drilled first into one eye, then the other. Once he had a wide-angle vision of a white room, one wallpapered. *See that wallpaper? Billy's hand. He loved things to be pretty.* A dark face bent over him. "Dixon?" Dave said, but it wasn't Dixon. He knew the name. Patek. A Swiss watch. That was what it was. Then everything was nothing for a long time. Or what seemed a long time.

Patel. That was the right name. The Pakistani doctor. Dave smiled and opened his eyes. Amanda stood by the bed. She wore a jacket too large in the shoulders, and a man's hat, domed, flat-brimmed. "Dave? How do you feel?" Nothing again for a long time.

Then he was riding through the rain in the unmarked police car driven by Samuels. He was gasping for breath. He was very sick. "I'm sorry," he said, "but I guess I'm going to pass out." And a voice beside him said, "It's okay, Dave. You're going to be okay."

He opened his eyes, and it wasn't Samuels, it was Cecil. He was holding Dave's hand. He turned his beautiful head to say to someone, "He's coming out of it." But he wasn't.

Kevin Nakamura grinned at him from the foot of the bed. The room was bright with sunshine. "Hey," he said, "I got the Valiant back all right." Then nurses crowded around in white. He was in a henhouse. He was four years old. His father had told him about all those eggs. Dave wanted the eggs. The chickens flapped and squawked around him. White feathers flew like snow. It was his last attempt at crime. No snow now. Blackness again. Then the faces beside the bed were Leppard's blunt black one, and that of his superior, Captain Ken Barker—steel-gray hair, heavy brow ridges, a broken nose.

Dave said, "I only dropped two."

Barker said, "You're a tough man to look out for."

"Stay home after this, please?" Leppard said. "You put yourself out on the streets, he's going to jump you again."

"I'll stay home when you've caught him," Dave said.

And that was all of that. The next faces were Madge Dunstan's handsome, horsey one, looking aggrieved, and Tom Owens's, with the odd yellow eyes. "Have a drink," Dave told them. "It'll cheer you up."

"I was the one who gave Dodge your card," Owens said.

"Jesus." Dave fought a tangle of tubes and wires, and struggled to sit up. His shoulder hurt, but the pain was dim, far off. They had drugged him half to death. Owens's bony face kept blurring and coming back into focus. Madge bent over Dave, trying to help him, poking and tugging at pillows. Dave reached out to Owens. "When?" he said. "When did you give it to him?"

"Day before he was killed," Owens said. "He came to me. Said a blackmailer was after him. He needed advice. You were the best advice I could give him."

Dave sagged back on the pillows. "Water, Madge? I'm so bloody dry." He opened his eyes. It was daytime. Beyond the window he saw the tops of tall palms bending in a wind. Rain was falling again. Madge held a glass of water to his mouth. He took a few small swallows. It tired him. "What the hell happened to me?"

"Anaphylactic reaction." Now a young man in white bent over him, bespectacled, balding, with a coppery moustache. He smelled of vitamin B. "To antibiotics. You didn't warn the emergency room staff."

"It never happened before," Dave said. "I didn't know."

"Well, now we all know." The doctor grinned. "And it won't happen again, will it?"

"I sincerely hope not," Dave said.

Cecil, too, wore a jacket too long and too wide in the shoulders, sleeves rolled halfway up the forearms, the shirt cuffs with them. Blowsy trousers, the extra material crumpled by a cloth belt cinched at his narrow waist. He looked ashamed, standing in the doorway of Dave's hospital room, the light of the busy hallway behind him, where food carts passed, the soles of shoes squeaked, medicine carts jingled, trays of dishes and glassware. "I'm sorry," he said, "I wasn't ready for it. It was just too gruesome."

Dave nodded. "You said that on the phone."

"They put me in a surgeon's gown and mask and cap."

Cecil came and sat by Dave's bed. "Took me to the ward. I found the room, but I couldn't go in."

"The gown and mask weren't to protect you." Carmen Lopez stepped out of the shadows into the circle of lamplight around the bed. She wore another neat, dark sweatshirt, jeans, jogging shoes. In the soft glow of the lamp, her face shone like a smooth brown wood carving. "It was to keep you from infecting them. You couldn't get nothing from them. Not just breathing. AIDS don't work that way."

"I know," Cecil said. "It wasn't that. I wasn't afraid of that. It was something else. I don't know the name of it. I couldn't make myself go in that room. Two of them in there—Tinker and one named Faircloth. Skeletons, Dave. Tinker's my age. He looked seventy. I couldn't go in."

"I'm sorry I sent you." Dave sat in the bed and pushed at the supper on his tray. "I wasn't thinking. When I have this need to know, sometimes I'm callous."

"Hell, you have a right to know," Cecil said. "I'm supposed to be a newsman." He snorted, shook his head in disgust. "I panicked. What I saw in ten seconds through that door— I'll never forget it. And I ran down the hall, tearing off the mask and cap and gown, and I got the hell out of there." He gave a bleak laugh at himself. "Rain never felt so good to me, so clean. I just stood there on the sidewalk outside old Juniper Serra and turned my face up and held out my hands and let it wash me, soak me."

"It's how everybody feels at first," Carmen said. "But it isn't sewage, you know, filth. It's just an animal you can't see, a virus that grabs hold of the T cells and kills them. A live thing in the blood. You have to remind yourself of that all the time."

Dave set the spun aluminum dome over his supper. It was bland, colorless. Hospital food. He wished he'd got Max to sneak him in something decent. But he wouldn't have felt like eating that, either. Not under these conditions. He said to Carmen, "It was good of you to go. What did Tinker say?"

"I told him how they all must have known the one who stabbed him—otherwise he couldn't have got so close to do it, otherwise they would have fought, or tried to fight." She smiled wanly. "You know, Art was feisty. Like a little *gallo*—what do you say, a fighting rooster? He had to be, where we grew up in Boyle Heights. He was small, and the boys called him names because he was pretty like a little doll, all right? And he learned to fight. He wouldn't let nobody stick him with a knife like that."

"Art was blind," Dave reminded her. "What did Tinker say?"

She moved her dark, thick eyebrows, lifted and let fall her chunky shoulders. "He don't know who it was. It could have been somebody Sean had sex with sometime. But Sean had sex with hundreds of men. He lived half his life at the baths. And he didn't stop there. He had sex in parks, alleys, cars, everyplace."

"It made it nice for Tinker," Cecil said.

Her laugh was sad. "He loved Sean. They started out together, came out together in junior high, okay? And Tinker, all he ever wanted was Sean O'Reilly. For the rest of his life, you know?" She sighed, trying to smile. "He could have been a priest, couldn't he? It was like that with him. Eternal love. He lays there now too weak to get up, spots all over him, infections wrecking him inside, weighs eighty pounds, okay? Dying. And it's love he talks about. How he loved Sean. How beautiful he was. He says he don't believe in God, but he wishes he did, so then he'd believe you don't die like a sheep or something, you go to heaven. He'd like to find Sean waiting for him in heaven."

"The men's room," Dave said.

She blinked, then gave another sad laugh. "Yeah, right. All he gave Tinker was grief and loneliness."

"And AIDS," Cecil said. "So Tinker doesn't know which of Sean's hundreds of tricks came back to kill him, right?"

"That was Sean's one kindness to him," Carmen said. "He never brought them home." She stood and went to the window to gaze into the rainy dusk. "And you know what Tinker says? I mean, he raved for a while, like I was Luke Skywalker, and we were in that spaceship. *Star Wars,* all right? There's parasites in his brain. He don't know what's happening, sometimes. But then he knew who I was again, and he told me, 'It wasn't Sean gave me AIDS. It was somebody a long time ago, years ago, when I thought I should live like Sean, and I went with maybe a dozen boys. I didn't like it. It made me hate myself, and I quit. But it was then I got AIDS. It stays inside you, waiting.' He looked at me, tears running down his face, shaking his poor head on the pillow, like a skull. 'It wasn't Sean,' he kept saying. 'I just know it wasn't Sean.'"

"Someone else wasn't so sure," Dave said. "The description of the skinny boy with long blond hair didn't bring anyone to mind?"

"Not to Tinker," Carmen said. "But Faircloth was listening. He had magazines all over his bed. He was cutting out pictures of naked boys and pasting them in a scrapbook."

"For future reference?" Cecil said. "What future?"

"Faircloth isn't going to die," Carmen said. "That's what he says." She looked at Dave. "He laid down the scissors, and he said, 'That sounds like Hoppy Wentworth.'"

"Good." Cecil stood up. "Where do we find him?"

"Sit down," Carmen said. "He died last Christmas."

9

"WHAT TELEVISION SHOWS you"—a pale-skinned, unshaven man named Rogers set a carton of books inside a yellow rental truck in a Van Nuys driveway—"is some poor woman whose husband was a druggie who used dirty needles and gave her AIDS." Rogers wore denim cutoffs, a sweaty tank top, and rubber sandals. He drew a hairy forearm across his forehead to wipe away sweat. "She's skin and bones, right? So feeble she can hardly talk. And she's leaving behind this brood of dear little children. Orphans. It's pathetic." Dave put him in his middle thirties. He was running to fat. Wind with a promise of rain in it stirred his thinning hair. "Made you want to cry. I did cry."

"Right," Dave said. "Moving. I saw it."

"And that newsmagazine piece?" Rogers hiked himself up into the truck that held furniture draped in blankets, plastic baskets of clothes, mattress and box spring against the walls, television set, stereo equipment, cartons of pots and pans, records, tapes, books. Rogers's voice came muffled from the truck. "About that wonderful doctor in Brooklyn, or someplace. The cover story. Damned good. But it's mostly about this lovely young Latino woman dying of AIDS. Contracted it from a bisexual lover seven years before she met her present husband. Beautiful, tragic young woman, right? Right." He jumped down out of the truck, grabbed one door and banged it closed, grabbed the other and banged it closed. "But is it women he really looks after most? No. Not in that area. It's druggies." He worked iron bolts to fasten the doors shut. "Which is also a warp." He faced Dave again, brushing his hands together. "Who really has AIDS? Gays, that's who. But they get shoved away inside the story, don't they? You just know the editor was quaking in his shoes when he faced the fact he had to mention who the ones are dying like flies from AIDS. Not pretty young women. Nasty, nasty gays."

"Now, are you sure that's it?" A middle-aged woman came down the walk. She brandished a newly bought floor mop like a weapon. She wore jeans, tennis shoes, sweatshirt, rubber gloves. A dish towel was tied over her hair. "Because I'm going to scrub and sterilize this house from top to bottom, and I don't want you coming back to pick up something you forgot, understand? You're out for good as of this minute."

"Me and my retroviruses," Rogers told her.

"Listen to him." The woman said this to Dave. She had knobby jaws and squinty eyes. "He jokes—about a thing like that. Spreads a deadly, disgusting disease through a house he rents from a decent, innocent person, and never says word one. Not word one." She blinked fury at Rogers. "Not brave enough to come out from the start and say what you and Frank Prohaska were to each other, oh, no. "We's just bachelors.'" Her thin mouth writhed over bright false teeth when she spoke the word. "Bringing women from your office here, making believe they meant something to you." She snapped at Dave, "Do you know what he is?"

"That's a complicated question," Dave said.

"Nothing complicated about it," she said. "A pervert— that's what. And Frank dying of that—that—filthy, slimy disease. In my house. And this one lying about it. Oh, it's just a cold, an upset stomach, an allergy. Ugh!"

"You loved our barbecues," Rogers said. "You and old Brad. All those free wine coolers. Sunday after Sunday."

"I want to throw up when I think of it," she said. "I ought to report you to the health department. I ought to call the police and have you locked up." She waved the mop in his face. "Get out. Get right out of here this minute, Don Rogers. I can't wait to forget you."

"Particularly since you owe me sixteen hundred bucks," Rogers said. "Don't say it, Flo. It's in the lease. I've got a copy. I'll take you to court. I'm a lawyer, remember?" He moved along to the cab of the truck, climbed up behind the wheel. The woman ran after him.

"When I send you a bill for the cleaning," she squawked up at him, "we'll see who owes who what."

Rogers slammed the cab door and started the engine. He snapped the parking brake loose and backed rapidly out the driveway. When the double rear wheels hit the street, he cramped the steering leftward, and when the truck turned, its cargo shifted. Glass and china smashed. Dave heard it as he got into the Jaguar at the curb. He drove after the truck. When it drew to a halt at a main cross street a few blocks on, he pulled alongside it, tapped his horn. Rogers looked out at him. Blankly. Then with recognition. A coffeeshop stood on an opposite corner—deep-eaved shake roof, thick beam ends, dark glass, rugged stone, planters rich with leafage. Dave pointed to the place. Rogers nodded. The traffic light changed. Rogers drove into the coffeeshop parking lot and found a place for the truck at the far end under a clump of ragged banana trees. Dave parked. They walked into the coffeeshop together.

Rogers ate as if eating was going to save him. A thick stack of flannel cakes swimming in butter and syrup. Eggs, sausage, bacon, toast. Pushing it desperately into his mouth. No time to talk. Scarcely time to breathe. The air came and went noisily through his nose. He stuffed his mouth and slurped coffee. His throat pumped. His eyes bulged.

Dave asked him, "Why Van Nuys, for God's sake?"

"Listen." Rogers mopped up his plate with a ragged scrap of toast. "It's a double bind." He gobbled the yolky toast, finished off his coffee, turned on the fake padded leather seat of the booth, and waved the coffee cup at a clutch of waitresses gossiping behind a counter. "You rent in West LA, and everybody knows you're a faggot. You move to Van Nuys, and try to blend in with the community. Flo was funny there. You think if we'd told her up front we were gay, she'd have rented to us? Forget it. So, you're there a week, and the talk starts. Ah." He set the cup in its saucer. A waitress in starchy brown and orange filled the cup and swept away their plates. When she'd gone, Rogers finished his thought: "'How come they're not married? No kids on the weekend? No friends but men?'" He patted his tank top, his cutoffs. "Shit. Have you got a cigarette?"

Dave took his pack out, pushed it across to Rogers, along with the lighter. Rogers lit up. Dave said, "So you enlisted the secretarial pool. Why don't you save yourself a lot of trouble and stop trying to please other people."

"Why? Look at Flo. She was okay, just as long as she didn't know, all right? We were friendly and if she had doubts she didn't let them get to her. We were good pay, always on time, kept the place up." He laughed a sorry little laugh. "You may find this hard to believe, but we had real good times. She loved Frank." His voice shook. "Jokes—about the soaps. They were like a couple high school kids when they started their shticks. Taking off the characters, the plots. It was a riot." He worked his mouth hard, biting his lips, but tears ran out of his eyes. He said, "Ah, shit, excuse me." He snatched paper napkins out of a shiny metal holder on the orange Formica table top and angrily wiped his eyes and pressed the wadded napkins to his mouth, and shook his head, unable to speak. Dave busied himself smoking, drinking coffee, gazing out the window past flower beds to the boulevard, where rain was falling again. Rogers laid the wadded paper napkins down. "I'm sorry.

I still can't get over it. It's too soon. He wasn't going to die for months and months. I was preparing myself for that. They have counseling sessions, you know, to get you ready. Not just the one that's going to die, the lovers, the families, whoever is going to be left behind." Rogers drew shakily on his cigarette, blew at his coffee, tried the coffee. "God damn it, I loved him so. I was so lucky to have him."

"How did he get AIDS?" Dave said.

"I didn't say he was perfect," Rogers said. "He was impulsive. He couldn't help it. I'm not made like that."

"Except about food," Dave said.

Rogers looked blank again, then laughed. "Oh, food. Yeah, right. Well, that was how Frank was about sex. I mean, he wouldn't go prowling. No, no. But if it cropped up, if it landed in his lap, he couldn't resist, you know?"

"How often did this happen?" Dave said.

"In West LA?" Rogers said. "Too often. You can't go around the corner to the 7-11 for a bag of croissants and a bottle of Tanqueray without some stranger putting the make on you. Or some neighbor out walking his dog." Rogers smoked for a moment, drank coffee, set the cup down. "Out here it was no problem. And we were very happy."

Dave fought to keep a straight face.

"We were. Really. Backyard barbecues and all. I mean, what faggot do you know who doesn't, in his heart of hearts, want to be just like Mr. and Mrs. Joe Doaks next door?" His voice wobbled again. He stabbed out the cigarette in a little tin ashtray. "Damn. We had time coming to us."

"Except Frank went back to West LA," Dave said.

Rogers's eyes pleaded with him. "Just that once."

"Once was all it took," Dave said. "Did you ever meet any of those pickups of his? For instance, a tall, skinny street kid, long blond hair tied back with a bandana?"

"A hippie?" Rogers gave a crooked smile. "No. Button-down collars were Frank's style. If the wristwatch didn't cost at least five hundred dollars, Frank wasn't interested.

And no long hair. Please. Disgusting. No, he liked people clean, squeaky clean."

"It's hard to be sure about that," Dave said.

Rogers laughed bleakly. "Isn't it just." His face crumpled again, and he pawed out for the napkin dispenser. "I miss him so. What's going to become of me?"

Dave said, "Don't cry. Answer my question."

Rogers uncovered his face. "No," he shouted. "I never met any of them. Who the hell is this kid? Why is he doing this crazy thing? Those men were all dying. What's the point? And why Frank, of all people? Why Frank?"

"And Art Lopez, and Sean O'Reilly, and Billy Bumbry, and Edward Vorse, and Drew Dodge. Why them? Did you know any of them? Did Frank Prohaska know them?"

"Not I. I already told the police." Rogers wiped his face again, blew his nose, wadded the napkins, laid the wad on the table. "I don't know them. I heard the names. Read them in the *Times,* saw them on television. Frank? If he knew them, he never said so to me. He would have said so. We told each other everything."

"Sure you did." Dave picked up the check.

"Give me that." Rogers grabbed for it. Dave held it away from him. And it seemed to him that for the first time in the hour and a half this encounter had lasted, Rogers registered that one of Dave's arms was in a sling. He frowned, dropped his hand to the tabletop. "What happened to you?"

"The blond kid I spoke of," Dave said, and pushed out of the booth, "tried to kill me, too. He missed."

"Dear God." Rogers lost some of his surliness. "I'm sorry. I didn't know. That's why you're poking around. I wish I could help."

Dave said, "You've got enough trouble. Forgive me for bothering you. Thanks for your time."

Rogers slid out of the booth. "Thanks for breakfast." Dave paid the check, and they pushed outdoors. "Rain," Rogers said disgustedly. "Just what I needed."

"Where are you moving to?" Dave said.

"My parents. The furniture goes in their garage. I'll let my car sit outside." He walked up the parking lot toward the yellow truck. The rain laid a quick bright surface on the tarmac. It washed over Rogers's sandals, but he didn't seem to notice. "I'll find an apartment. I just need time. Flo wasn't about to give me that."

"No. Well, it's good you have a roof to stop under," Dave said. "Your parents will be some comfort to you."

Hand on the truck door, Rogers turned back. "Are you kidding? They don't know about me. Luckily, the TV news ignored me when Frank was killed. My parents never even knew Frank and I lived together. When I simply had to have them over, he'd take all his stuff and hide out at a friend's." Rogers climbed into the truck. "Believe me, my parents won't be any comfort. I hope to God I can keep from crying."

"Explain," Dave said. "Give them a chance to help."

"Be serious," Rogers said, and started the truck.

When Dave swung the Jaguar into the street, he saw Samuels get into an unmarked car down the block.

10

THE MONTE VERDE rose out of dark old trees on the steep hills above the Sunset Strip, a gray stone tower, built in the 1920s, the setting of legends. Had John Barrymore, Greta Garbo, Anna Sten really lived here? Was this where young Mary Astor had bedded down with George S. Kaufman? Did it matter? Did it matter if a renowned German director had been shot full of holes by his dandelion-haired twelve-year-old mistress among his vases of peacock feathers on the ninth floor? If that French comedian had hanged himself in a harness of straps and chains in the penthouse? If two teenage boys had really turned a Romanian concert pianist's Bechstein into his coffin one moonlit summer night? Dave had forgotten half the stories he'd heard about the Monte Verde, but when he pushed in through the bronze and glass doors out of the clammy drip of the funereal cypresses at the entrance, the vast high tomb of the lobby made him believe the ones he remembered. He'd never set foot in a place that felt so haunted. He made for elevator doors, far across the lobby.

"Sir." The voice came from behind a carved counter between two Gothic pillars. "Who did you want to see? I'll telephone and tell them you're here." The speaker was a six-foot man-child in clothes even wider in the shoulders and blowsier in the trousers than Cecil's and Amanda's. His hair was shaved on the sides and spiky on top and dyed blue. He wore a blue glass earring, blue war paint above his blue eyes, and he held a telephone receiver at the ready.

"Milford Stein," Dave said. The place echoed the name.

"And you are?" the young man said.

"Dave Brandstetter. I'm a private investigator. Mr. Stein isn't expecting me. Tell him it's about the death of Edward Vorse."

The young man put down the phone. "He won't see you."

"Shall we let him decide that?" Dave said.

"The man is an emotional wreck. He can't take any more." Dave turned and headed for the elevators again.

"You need a key to operate the elevators," the desk clerk said. "And to get the key away from me, you'll have to kill me." That surprised Dave, and he turned and stared at the young man. He was holding a revolver, a .38 by the look of it, and new. He was pointing it at Dave's chest. "I'm sorry about the uniform, but a person has to draw the line somewhere. I am a security guard. I am licensed to use this, and trained to use it."

"I just want to ask Mr. Stein a question," Dave said.

"Then telephone ahead," the clerk said, "or write a letter. Make an appointment. Have Mr. Stein leave word with this desk when you're expected." He smiled. His teeth showed braces. Dave wondered when he was going to have his twenty-first birthday. The child said, "All right? No hard feelings? Reasonable? Sensible? Businesslike?"

"Just like the gun." Dave went out under the dripping trees again. He stood on the cracked long curve of driveway for a minute, then headed down it. Not to unlock the Jaguar and drive off. To find Samuels and have Samuels lean on Boy Blue with the authority of the LAPD. But a tour bus came groaning up the drive. Dave stepped back into wet shrubbery to let it pass, then stood watching as it creaked to a hulking halt at the entrance, breathing out white exhaust into the drizzle.

The doors flapped open, and passengers began to climb down—well-dressed old people, most of them women wrapped in flowered plastic raingear. Laughing and chattering and giving little whoops about the rain, they hurried inside through the double doors. Dave climbed the drive again and stepped in among them, pulling off his Irish tweed hat so his white hair showed. He kept to the side of the crowd away from the desk, and turned the collar of his trenchcoat up to hide his face from Boy Blue, who greeted the group cheerily, and hurried to unlock the elevator doors. The crowd was big enough to fill two cars. Boy Blue opened both shafts. Dave squeezed into the second car, his lungs filling with gusts of English lavender from the Disneyland-happy old ladies.

Milford Stein's floor was the tenth. Dave hung back, letting the hallways empty. When the last merry bye-bye faded, and the last door closed with oaken solidity on the carpet-hushed corridors, he knocked at number 1008. Stein's horn-rimmed glasses looked too heavy for him. The eyes behind the thick lenses were large and brown and filled with sorrow. They made him look like a child, though his hair and skin were gray, and his face creased and craggy. He wore a hand-knit cotton sweater and well-worn wide-wale corduroy trousers. When he heard Dave's name and the name of Edward Vorse, he stepped back and made a mute gesture that invited Dave inside. He closed the door and reached, offering to take Dave's coat.

Dave said, "I won't stay. The boy on the desk downstairs made it plain you don't want to be disturbed."

Stein smiled faintly. "He acts like my mother." Stein plainly hadn't used his voice for a while. It was scratchy. He cleared his throat. "Do stay. Have a drink."

The room was crowded with antique sofas, chairs, tables, cabinets. Dave couldn't make out in the dimness—the walls of the Monte Verde were thick, the windows narrow—

whether the pieces were any good or not. Dark oil paintings in heavy gilt frames glowered on the walls. Stein was a set decorator for the studios. They didn't make a lot of period movies anymore. Did Stein feel comfortable anywhere but at home, nowadays? Stein opened doors on a tall cabinet far away. There came the faint chink of glass. He said: "Please sit down. What can I bring you?"

Dave shed the coat and hat. "Scotch, thanks." The stuffing of the wing chair he chose was lumpy. The velvet was threadbare, a condition cherished in today's market. He couldn't make out the color. Whatever it was, it had been darker a century ago. He took the glass Stein handed him, cut glass, lead crystal by the weight of it, and of the best workmanship—a man could shave on the edges. Stein sat down with his drink in a wing chair opposite. "The police," he said, "asked me all about Eddie and his associates. A Lieutenant Leppard. A fancy dresser." Stein smiled faintly. His tone grew ironic. "I couldn't tell him all about Eddie, could I? Like, for example, that Eddie had AIDS. What is it they say, the wife is always the last to know? I believed what I wanted to believe, didn't I? And let the questions go. I knew he was tricking around." Stein shrugged miserably. "I did my best to ignore it. I wanted him to be happy." Stein got up to find a chased silver cigarette box, to hold it out for Dave to take a cigarette, to take one himself, to set the box down again, to light Dave's cigarette and his own, to resume his seat. "You're a distinguished man in your profession. A celebrity. What brings you to my humble door about Eddie?"

Keeping it brief, Dave told him about finding Drew Dodge's body, and about being jumped in the dark by the knifer who'd killed Dodge. And maybe Eddie. "But something's out of kilter. I don't have AIDS. The police think all his victims knew him. I didn't. He was a tall, skinny street kid with long blond hair tied back with a bandana. Young, eighteen, maybe less. What I came to ask you is, did Eddie Vorse know anyone like that? Did you ever see them together? Ever meet him?"

"Only one of Eddie's little playmates fits that description," Stein said, and tapped cigarette ash into a cut-glass olive dish. "And he fits it perfectly. Yes, I met him. I didn't like him. He was one of those I made Eddie's life hell about. Trash. He had no sense of fitness, Eddie didn't. Or self-preservation, either—mine or his. I fed, sheltered, clothed him, gave him all the pocket money he wanted. But that punk brought cocaine here. To my apartment. Making me responsible. I could be arrested, I could lose my career. I'd told Eddie to be happy—but no drugs, all right? Then I walk in and find the two of them hunched over that table, snorting up the stuff with cocktail straws. I took a deep breath"—Stein acted this out now—"and blew it all over the room. I grabbed Rapunzel by the hair, dragged him to the door, and literally"—Stein raised a foot in scuffed tan suede—"kicked him out."

Dave grinned. "I'm sorry I missed it."

"I don't look it," Stein said, "but I'm strong. Slight, as they say, but wiry. You want his name, don't you?"

"If you please." Dave nodded.

"Let's see. It's been some time." Stein frowned and blinked at the shadowy ceiling. "Muir-Mure something. No. No. Damn." He jumped up out of the chair and paced, scowling, snapping his fingers. He stopped and gazed out one of the narrow rainy windows for a moment. He turned back, smiling. "Of course. Moorcock. How could I forget a name like that? I thought when Eddie spoke of him, "Demure cock," and wondered what the shy thing would look like." He came back to his chair and sat down happily and drank off the rest of his whisky. "First name? Michael, of course. God, how original people are, naming children. Pity I'm gay. I wouldn't give a child a hopeless first name like Michael. When there's one in every house on the block already? I'd read the entire *Dictionary of National Biography* through for a name before I'd saddle my child with Michael."

"The original was an archangel," Dave said.

"Guardian of the Jews," Stein said. "I know. Well, not this one. I'm not surprised he killed six people."

"I'm not sure about that," Dave said. "But I'd like to ask him. Where will I find him?"

Stein got out of his chair. "Eddie kept an address book." He had his own glass in his hand, and he took Dave's. He went off to the towering cabinet again. "Of course," he called across the vastness of the gloomy room, "he didn't list all his tricks in it. That would have required seven stout volumes." Glass chimed again. "But he confessed to me that Demure Cock had held a fascination for him for weeks—until I broke them up." Stein moved to another corner of the room. Hollow rattlings suggested he'd opened and closed a drawer. When he brought the new drinks, a leather-bound book was tucked under his arm. He set Dave's drink down, and handed him the book. Dave took out his reading glasses, found the *M* listings in the book— the handwriting was studied, a schoolboy try at Italic calligraphy—and there was *Mike Moorcock* and a telephone number. He closed the book, put the glasses away.

"Excuse an indelicate question," he said. "You don't have to answer it. But didn't you know about AIDS when Eddie was chasing around, tricking with strangers? Didn't you worry that he might get it, that you might?"

"I warned Eddie. What else could I do? As for me?" Stein gave a laugh. "Oh, my dear. I only do safe sex. I never knew there was any other kind until I was almost thirty—can you believe it? Once or twice I tried to oblige with the variations, but it didn't take." His smile was sad and wry. "That must explain why I was so satisfying as a lover to poor Eddie."

"Don't blame yourself." Dave peered into the shadows. "May I use your phone?"

Stein brought it to him, set it on the table, left the room. The phone was a fancy contraption of ebony and gilt. He laid the receiver aside and with his good hand turned a silent gold and ivory dial to reach Ray Lollard. An old friend in a powerful job at Pacific Bell, Ray queened it in a handsome restored mansion of turrets and stained glass on Adams Boulevard. In a refurbished stable building behind the house, he kept a wild-haired, antic young potter named Kovaks. They made an odd couple. Ray and Dave had met in high school, and still saw each other now and then. And Ray always matched up scrappy telephone numbers with addresses and names when Dave needed him to. Now, receiver in his good hand, Dave got Moorcock's address from him.

"What's it about?" he asked. And Dave told him of the knifing deaths of five young men with AIDS in the past three weeks, and of his finding of Drew Dodge's body under his oak tree. Lollard drew a shocked breath. "Dave, no. Let the police handle it. It's too dangerous. You'll end up in the hospital again."

"Thanks, but I've already been in the hospital and out. Someone like Moorcock jumped me in the dark and tried to run a knife into my heart—like the others. Luckily, he only cut my shoulder."

"Dave," Lollard wailed, "when are you going to realize you are no longer a young man? What are you planning now—to go confront this creature in his den?"

"Don't worry," Dave said. "I'll have the police right behind me. I can't seem to shake them."

"And a good thing too," Lollard said strictly. "You need somebody looking out for you. You've taken leave of your senses. When can we have dinner?"

"When you stop dieting," Dave said.

"Oh, that's over with. I fell from grace months ago."

"Good," Dave said. "When I'm through with this case, I'll ring you. I'll have a bucket of raw meat to toss to Kovaks, too. Fresh, juicy bones. You tell him."

"He'd pace his cage all night. You be careful, now. I don't want that phone call to come from the morgue."

"I'll be careful," Dave said, and placed the overwrought receiver back on its hooks. He got to his feet, put on the

Irish hat. Stein came back into the room. "Thank you," Dave told him. "I'll go see if I can find Moorcock."

Stein frowned. "Shouldn't you leave it to the police?"

"I don't want to waste their time." Dave fumbled, trying to get the coat across his shoulders. Stein helped him. Dave said, "After all, there's more than one stringy child with long hair running the streets at night, cruising, hustling, peddling drugs, peddling disease." The coat felt secure now. He moved toward the door. "I'm grateful for your help."

"I'm grateful you came." Stein walked with him and opened the door. "It was good to talk to someone human."

Dave stopped in the doorway and looked at him. "I went into mourning once, long ago. The man I'd lived with for twenty-two years died of cancer. Shutting myself away only made it worse. It didn't begin to get better until I went back to work."

Stein pushed the heavy glasses up on his nose and used his woebegone smile again. "Thank you." He shook Dave's hand. "Maybe I'll try that."

11

NOVELLO STREET CLIMBED steeply north from Franklin Avenue, east of Vine. It was lined on both sides by white stucco apartment buildings. Golden rays of slanted sunlight shone on the west-facing fronts now. The rain clouds had torn apart so that there could be a sunset. What Dave glimpsed of it between buildings and through the high, sagging strands of power and telephone lines was gaudy. The blacktop of the street was still wet. So was the canted gray concrete of the sidewalks.

The address he wanted marked a two-story motel. Its flaking painted sign read HAVEN HOUSE and, in smaller letters *Youth Outreach of Our Savior's Church Hollywood.* On the sidewalk below the sign, a lanky young woman used a roller to try to paint out graffiti—FAGS CAUSE AIDS KILL ALL FAGS. The lettering was ragged and very black. The white paint the woman used wasn't covering it well.

Dave eased the Jaguar into a space at the curb. It took only two tries. He was getting good with just one arm. He pushed coins into a bent meter, and walked down to the woman. She wore a navy blue watch cap, gray turtleneck, blue windbreaker jacket, black jeans, white tennis shoes. She tipped paint from a pail into a pan and, when Dave stopped beside her, straightened and smiled ruefully.

"This is the fifth time in two weeks," she said. "It isn't hatred, not really. It's fear."

"Those two keep close company," Dave said.

The woman dipped the roller in the pan of paint, rolled it a little there, lifted it and swiped again at the angry words. "In the end, I'll just sandblast. But that's expensive. We have to stretch a meager budget very, very thin, as things are. I'll wait till the panic dies down."

"That could take years," Dave said.

"They're working on cures," she said.

"Right. One of them kills the virus, but it's toxic to the bone marrow. You have to have your blood replaced every three weeks. AIDS doesn't kill you—anemia does."

"It takes forever for paint to dry in this weather," she said, and rested the roller in the pan, its long handle against the wall. "You're talking about AZT. But they've got others."

"One of them's a dandy," Dave said. "It kills the T-cells while it kills the retrovirus. There's no hope in that, Sister."

"Jan Crofoot." She worked up another smile and held out a painty hand. Dave shook it. "But it's not sister. We're Protestants. Rome is still nervous about homosexuality. We got over that in the sixties. It caused an awful ruckus, but charity won out in the end." She touched the wall where the spray-painted message still showed through. She rubbed the ends of her fingers with her thumb. Her mouth twitched. "Not all Protestants, of course. Our denomination, and a few others. No, no." She laughed sadly and shook her head. "Not the evangelicals. Talk about hatred. How that bunch can hate. It's ignorance, you know. Just ignorance."

"You're a charitable lady," Dave said.

"It comes with the territory. What can I do for you?"

Dave told her his name and showed her his license. He told her about Drew Dodge and about the boy who had knifed him.

"It may have been Michael Moorcock. I traced him to this address because he called your phone number his."

Jan Crofoot was in the middle of a stroke with the roller. She stopped and frowned at Dave. "Recently? You mean in the midst of these terrible stabbings?"

"Maybe at the end of them," Dave said. "I hope so."

"No, I mean, did he give this number recently? Because that makes no sense. He left here"—she hesitated, muddling the roller in the paint pan again—"how long ago? Surely it's been months."

"Do you keep records?" Dave said.

She looked up and down the street. It was deserted. She stood the roller in the pan again, handle angled against the wall. "Come inside," she said, and led the way. The former motel was L-shaped, the long side at right angles to the street, the short side at the far end of the lot. Where cars used to park stood tents—olive drab, from some Army surplus store. There was also a green- and white-striped canvas marquee, the kind set up for garden parties on tubular framework. From the fringed, scalloped edges of the roof hung sheets of clear plastic, of green plastic trash bags sliced to double their width, fixed with safety pins, clothespins, staples. Within, Dave glimpsed sleeping bags, backpacks, strewn clothing, and huddled young people.

"The units are filled to overflowing." Crofoot waved a hand at the encampment. "The police and health people don't like this. They make us dismantle it every now and then, but we put it up again as soon as they're out of sight. They can't be everyplace." She used a pair of keys in a pair of locks to open a door marked OFFICE.

"Don't they fine you?" Dave said. "Don't the fines stretch that budget even thinner?"

"Then we call on friends." Crofoot moved through random stacks of cartons, some of them with open flaps, files inside, unsorted papers. Some cartons came from grocery warehouses, canned chili, canned hash, sardines. Loaves of bread in white wrappers were dumped in a corner, sacks of onions, potatoes, oranges. A stem of bananas lay on the desk Crofoot now edged behind. The shut-up room air smelled of bananas. She lifted the stem with an effortful grunt and held it for a grimacing moment, to say, "Care for a banana?" Dave shook his head, and she lowered the stem to the floor, out of sight. "We call on friends who drive expensive imported cars." Her smile at Dave was sly. "They always come through in emergencies." Her laugh was self-conscious. She rubbed her hands, sat down, pulled toward a double file box of three-by-five cards. "Now, let's see—Michael Moorcock. He may still be in the active file"—the paint-stained fingers riffled through the cards— "because office help is catch-as-catch-can."

"What about the boys out there?" Dave said.

"Ah, well, there are drawbacks to that," Crofoot said. "Most of them can barely read. Alphabetical order—what's that? And then they're—some of them—shall we say, a little short on probity. For sneaky reasons, cards are apt to be misplaced, lost, let's say, forever."

"Who do you get?" Dave looked toward the door.

"Street boys, sometimes on drugs, sometimes robbed and beaten and exploited in various ways because they're gay or country-dumb or scared and lost and hungry. Not just kids—men sometimes. Early on, things were co-ed, but all kinds of trouble arose from that. You can imagine."

"I can imagine all kinds of trouble arising from this," Dave said. "What about weapons, knives, guns, what about drugs and violence and coercion and the rest? You don't make good little Christians out of them all?"

"We don't even try. We feed them, give them a place to sleep, a place to shower. We get them medical attention at clinics and hospitals when they need it. Drug counseling. Therapy if the problems are mental or emotional. We hunt up their parents if they're very young. We try to protect them from exploitation on the streets, and from the arbitrariness of the law, if we think it will leave them worse off instead of better."

"We?" Dave said. "I hope you've got a lot of help."

Crofoot smiled wearily. "I confess—it's mostly me."

"But they're not all gay?" Dave said.

"Oh, by no means. Ah, here we are." She pulled a card from the little wooden drawer. "Michael Moorcock." She blinked at the card a moment, shook her head, held the card out to Dave. "Gone, left no forwarding."

"But there's a date here." Dave put on reading glasses and squinted at the card. "December tenth, last year."

"I told you it had been a while," she said. "I remember Michael." She pawed around in a welter of papers on the desk and found a cigarette pack. When she lit a cigarette from the pack, the smell of the smoke was strong. Turkish, Dave thought. "Tall, slender boy, very fair hair that he wore long, down to his shoulders."

Dave handed back the card. "Did he also carry a knife?" He tucked his glasses into a jacket pocket.

"We don't search them." Crofoot peered into the file drawer, slipped the card back in place. "He may have owned a knife." She pushed the little drawer shut. "But it wasn't the knife that got him into trouble. It was drugs. A boy came to me and said Moorcock was selling crack." She laughed bleakly. "To raise a little money for Christmas, I suppose."

"Did you confront him about it?" Her cigarette smoke was tough to breathe. He tried to make out the printing on the crumpled yellow pack on the desk. Could it be Fatima? Did they still make those? "Is that why he left?"

"Yes. If I didn't act promptly and strictly about drugs," Crofoot said, "we'd be in deep trouble here." She pulled off the white cap and ruffled her thick, honey-colored hair with her fingertips, as if her scalp itched. "The police would close us once and for all. I tell them, 'Bring drugs in here, and there won't be a Haven House anymore—no free food, no place to sleep.'" She smoothed her hair and put the cap on again. "I encourage them to snitch. I don't much like myself for that."

"Don't feel bad," Dave said. "You were right about Moorcock. I have a witness that he was into cocaine."

Before she could answer, knuckles rapped the door. She called, "Come in." A teenage boy poked his head in. On his shiny, shaven scalp someone had painted an ancient Celtic spiral in red and gold. Also on his flat cheeks. "We straightened up the storage room like you asked. Can we take this stuff now?"

Crofoot said yes, and the skinhead came inside, followed by a short, black youth in an embroidered cap whose bright colors had grown grimy. His caftan needed washing, too. It was of gaudy cotton print. Rain was falling again, and the long garment clung to him. His body was a tidy sculpture. The boys picked up cartons and staggered out with them, wheezing, laughing.

Crofoot went and closed the door. She said to Dave, "I hope today's volunteer cook doesn't ring to tell me her babysitter has let her down." She glanced worriedly at an old black telephone that squatted on the desk. "Cooking is a chore I can live without. Oh, I do it," she added hastily, "but not, I fear, with Christian cheerfulness." She read her watch and sighed. "It looks like the deadline has arrived."

"I've cooked meals with one arm before," Dave said, "but not for a hundred hungry kids."

Crofoot smiled. "Thanks, I'll manage. She'll no doubt be along. The freeways are wet. That means traffic jams. I'll just get things started for her." She opened the door.

The boys came threading their way through the tents from which radio music blared, shrieking guitars, thudding drums. When the boys were inside the office, Dave closed the door and asked the skinhead, "Did you know Mike Moorcock when he lived here?" He looked the same question at the black boy.

They turned to Crofoot, as if to say, "Who is this? Do we have to answer him?"

Crofoot busied herself putting out her cigarette, and Dave said, "Did he tell you where he was going when he left?"

"What for do you want to know?" The black lad plucked the thin, soaked cloth away from his crotch. He was embarrassed. He had nothing on under the caftan. "You police?"

"Have you seen him since?" Dave said.

"He peddles crack along Franklin, around Wilcox," the white boy said in a bored voice.

He picked up cartons. "He did. He got busted. That's what I heard."

"Onions?" the black boy said to Crofoot. "We got those?"

"In the corner." Crofoot pointed.

"When did he get busted?" Dave said.

"Last weekend. I guess nobody bailed him out. I go past there all the time. I haven't seen him." He tottered toward Dave, thin arms straining with the weight of the cartons. "You want to open the door, please?"

Dave opened the door. The skinhead went out into the rain. The black kid came laden with net sacks of onions. "Cook, she say nothing taste right without onions." He followed the skinhead off between the tents.

"Ah." Crofoot glowed. "The cook's come."

Dave grinned. "Saved from an awful fate, right? I'll go. Thanks for your help."

Out on the sidewalk in the dying light, he saw that someone had made off with paint, pan, roller. He didn't take the bad news back inside. FAGS CAUSE AIDS KILL ALL FAGS still showed through. Bullets struck the words now. He heard the whine of bullets past his ears. He saw the stucco shatter and fly away in fragments. He dropped to the sidewalk. Two more bullets hit the wall. Bits of stucco stung his face. Someone shouted. Dave got carefully to his feet. Across the street, Samuels in his pale coat ran away between buildings, gun in his hand. Past him, Dave glimpsed a skinny, ragged kid, running like hell, long blond hair streaming. The light was poor, but didn't it have to be Moorcock? Whoever it was dodged from sight at a building corner, dodged back, fired a gun. Samuels fell down. Dave ran back into the court of Haven House, clutching the arm in the sling. The door to the office stood open. The boy with the shaved head came out, a gunnysack of potatoes balanced on a bony shoulder. Crofoot walked behind him, talking. When she saw Dave, her mouth closed, and her eyes opened wide. Over the shriek of radios, Dave shouted to her, "Phone the police. There's been a shooting. Tell them an officer is down."

12

SOPHIE SAMUELS WAS plump and pale like her husband.
She wore a yellow sweater, faded blue jeans, jogging shoes.
And she held on her lap a plump, pale child of maybe
three. The child slept with its head of pale curls nestled
under Sophie Samuels's chin, and its thumb in its mouth.
Beside mother and child on the couch where they sat lay
the mother's pink raincoat and the child's very small red
plaid one. The mother stared over the baby's head at a
pottery jar of flowers that stood on a coffee table strewn
with tattered magazines and empty paper cups. The place
was an alcove for anxious people to wait in off a hospital
corridor near the rooms where surgery was done.

Dave waited there, too, smoking, trying to remember
not to smoke. Jeff Leppard wore tweeds again, and found
it hard to sit still. He kept jumping up and walking down
the corridor to its end, and walking back again. Now and
then, his eyes met Dave's. Nothing friendly was in their
look. If Dave had stayed home and minded his own business,
Samuels wouldn't have been shot. Leppard had let himself
say this much to Dave in the rainy areaway between those
two scabby apartment buildings on Novello Street while
blue uniforms in clear plastic raincoats beat the

neighborhood searching for the suspect, and ambulance attendants hustled Samuels off on a gurney in his bloody fly-front coat. Leppard was wrong to say it, and he knew it, and said no more. But Dave didn't blame him. He also didn't blame himself. He hadn't asked for Samuels to guard him. Or anyone else.

Samuels's partner, Dugan, had come and gone earlier. The surgery was taking a long time. It was Dugan who brought the flowers, hoping they'd speak for him. A leathery older cop, his husky voice stammered when he tried to express his concern to Sophie. She'd scarcely looked at him. She'd sat staring at the flowers. Captain Ken Barker arrived later, and was better when it came to finding the words, the tone to talk to the frightened wife, to lend her comfort, reassurance, a sense that someone cared. Still, she'd said little in return, murmured thanks, a wan try at a smile. "He's only thirty-two," she said. "Too young to die."

"Who said anything about dying?" Barker said.

"He didn't want to be a cop," she said. "He wanted to be a lawyer." Tears ran down her cheeks, she chewed her lip. "But he wasn't smart enough."

Barker laughed gentry. "Neither are most lawyers. Don't cry." He found tissues in a pocket and bent and dried her tears. "He's only gun shot. It hurts but not forever."

She nodded tearily. "Thank you for the flowers."

Barker turned to Dave. "Whoever it was," he said, "it wasn't Michael Moorcock. He's in jail, waiting trial for peddling crack. He was in jail the night Drew Dodge was killed, still there when you were attacked at your house. We don't know where he was when Eddie Vorse was killed, but we didn't find any knife among Moorcock's possessions."

Dave nodded glumly. "Stein's description fit, so did Crofoot's, but nothing ever comes that easy, does it?"

"You'd hate it if it did," Barker said.

"Not really," Dave said. "I'm tired. I'd like to get it over with."

"Tell me about it," Barker said. He rubbed his broken nose, moved his blocky shoulders restlessly, looked up the corridor. "I could use a drink. And you sure as hell look as if you could."

Dave glanced at the young woman. "I can't go. She's got to think the way Leppard thinks—that this is my fault. I'll stay here until it's over."

"What's the prognosis?" Barker said.

"Fifty-fifty. He took it in the chest, almost in the sternum. Maybe it got his heart. Maybe not."

Then the double doors marked SURGERY pushed open, and a tired-looking tall man in a green surgical gown came out, pulling a green mask down so he could show a weary smile to Sophie Samuels. "It took some fancy needlework, but he'll be all right," he said. "Good as new." He glanced at Ken Barker. "Captain—you'll have him back on the job in six weeks." He pulled off the green cap. His gray hair was tangled and sweaty. "What happened to bulletproof vests?"

Barker said, "Nobody was expecting bullets on this assignment." He looked grimly at Dave.

The double doors of the surgery room slammed open, and a gurney was pushed out into the hallway by green-clad help. One of them held high a plasma bag. They wheeled the gurney swiftly away. Sophie Samuels gave a cry. "Joey!" She struggled to her feet, made awkward by the burden of the child. She took steps, meaning to catch up with the gurney, but the surgeon stopped her. "You can see him when he's in post-op. For just a few minutes, all right?"

"Thank you." She didn't look at him. She looked at the gurney, disappearing into an elevator. "Oh, God." She sank down on the stiff little couch again and began to weep. Not from worry now. From relief.

Leppard came down the corridor from somewhere. He stopped and stood over her. "Will you be all right?" he said. "Have you a ride home? Is there someone to stay there with you tonight?"

"I have my car." Sophie was making a soggy wad of the tissues Barker had given her. Sniffling, she looked up and gave Leppard a wet, wobbly smile. "My parents are coming. From Simi Valley." Blinking back tears, she read her watch. "They'll probably be at the apartment before us." She kissed the sleeping child and shook it gently. "Wake up, Pepper. We're going to see Daddy now." She set Pepper on his small feet, worked at getting his limp short arms into the sleeves of the little plaid coat. The child kept nodding, leaning drowsily against her knees, eyes shut.

Leppard crouched to help out. He said, "That's quite a name, Pepper." He tickled the pudgy little tummy, and Pepper giggled. "That's all right," Leppard told Sophie. "I'll carry him." He took the baby up on his arm.

Sophie snatched her own raincoat off the couch, and hurried away up the corridor after him. At the elevators, she remembered, turned, waved to Barker, smiling. "Thank you, Captain," she called. She didn't call anything to Dave. He didn't expect her to.

He got heavily to his feet, and said to Barker, "I think I can use that drink now."

A car with its lights off sat half in the drainage ditch on Horseshoe Canyon Trail when Dave reached home. He made out two figures seated inside the car. If there had been only one, he'd have worried. He jounced the Jaguar down onto the bricks. Cecil's van sat in its old familiar place. He moaned inwardly. He wasn't up to a confrontation tonight. The drinks with Barker at Max Romano's, and the good food afterward, had left him in a mood to listen to music and drift off to sleep. It had been a long day. He parked beside the van and clambered out. A man from the unlighted car stood at the trail's edge. He said: "Leppard sent us. I'm Officer Gregory. My partner's Munroe. We'll be here all night if you need us. Don't worry if you hear us walking around. That's part of the drill."

"Thanks," Dave said, locked the Jaguar, and walked across rain-matted leaves on the bricks, around the end of the front building. The cookshack was dark. He hoped Cecil had fed himself. Cooking he was no more in the mood for now than a confrontation. He liked the idea of cooking right this minute as much as Crofoot liked it all the time. The back building was lighted. Not the front.

He unlocked the door of the front building, a broad, heavy door of thick glass panes clinched in strong wood—switched on lamps, crossed thickly carpeted floor, down steps, up steps to the stereo rig. He peered through reading glasses into little drawers of cassettes, rattling their brittle plastic cases, filing through them, seeking quiet music, settling on Miles Davis ballads.

He dropped the cassettes in a jacket pocket and left the front building. When he stepped into the back building, he didn't see Cecil. A lamp glowed on a table at one end of the long corduroy couch that faced the fireplace, and that was all. He walked down the room to hang hat and coat on the rack by the bar. "Whatever it is," he called, "I'd rather we talked about it down here." He poured brandy into two small snifters.

"You sure?" Cecil said from the sleeping loft.

Dave looked up. Cecil was naked. That had figured to happen, sooner or later. Dave carried the brandies to the couch. "Put your clothes on, please," he said.

"You didn't ask if I've told Chrissie," Cecil said.

"If you had, you wouldn't be trying desperate measures," Dave said. "There wouldn't be any need."

Cecil muttered and vanished from the rafter-shadowy light. Dave heard the whisper of cloth as he dressed. He came down the raw pine plank steps barefoot, carrying shoes and socks in his hand. He brought these to the couch, plumped down grumpily, bent forward to put them on. Dave sat at the other end of the couch, tasted his brandy, lit a cigarette. "Where is Chrissie?" he said.

"Braille Institute. This mine?" Cecil stretched an arm for the snifter Dave had set on the raised brick hearth. "Some kind of event happening there tonight." He glanced at the elaborate black watch on his wrist. "I have to pick her up at ten o'clock. I waited a long time for you. Where have you been?"

"Max's," Dave said, "with Ken Barker. I hope you ate." Cecil sipped the brandy. "I had something else in mind."

"Forget it," Dave said. "To make that easier, let me tell you about my day." He told it. "He got away. It took them hours to patch Samuels up, but they say he'll be all right. I wonder why the change of weapons—knife to gun?"

"Maybe it wasn't the same cracker," Cecil said.

"Looked the same, moved the same, angular but girlish."

"Some of us can't help that." Cecil touched his mouth with the brandy again and frowned. "What's his thinking? Put them out of their misery? Friends he knew. Can't bear to see them suffer. Is that why they let him get so close?"

"There was a spray-painted slogan on the front wall of Haven House," Dave said. "Crofoot was trying to paint it out. 'FAGS CAUSE AIDS. KILL ALL FAGS.'"

"Oh, wow." Despair was in Cecil's voice.

"When Baby shot at me," Dave said, "he hit those words."

"Stay home, Dave," Cecil said. "Please. Barker's got half the police department on it. Let them catch him. Don't go out there making yourself a target. No more, all right?" He drank off the brandy, set down the glass, rose. "I have to go. Take me forty minutes from here to Braille Institute." He bent, kissed Dave's mouth, made for the door. At the door he turned back. "You be all right alone here?"

"I'm not alone," Dave said. "They're risking the lives of two more officers to guard me. Out front."

"Good," Cecil said, and left.

The front of the Tiberius Baths was gray stucco, the forms of Roman columns and arches molded shallowly into it. Spotlight from police cars jamming Melrose Avenue glared on the pillars and arches and the plastered-up windows of the place. Light strips on the roofs of the police cars winked fitfully, red, amber, white. Police officers stood around in clumps among the cars. Some of the officers wore bulky protective vests and crash helmets and cradled rifles in their arms. It was a scene from a bad dream.

Officers Gregory and Munro had brought Dave here. They had wakened him by banging on the door of the rear building while Miles Davis played "Someday My Prince Will Come" softly through the stereo rig on the sleeping loft under the starlit skylight and Dave was drifting off to sleep, forgetting the ache in his shoulder, the day's alarms and excursions. He had moaned, flapped into a corduroy robe, limped down the stairs, unbolted the door, scowled at the two young uniforms, growled at them. Gregory stammered.

"Sorry to bother you, but we just got a call from the Lieutenant. Down in Hollywood. They've got the knifer, the one that tried to kill you, the one that killed all the AIDS victims? They've got him cornered. The lieutenant thought you'd like to be there when they bring him out. He said for us to drive you, if you want."

"I want," Dave said. "I'll get some clothes on."

When they reached the block where the action was, Munro had to thread the unmarked car between television news vans, had to tap his horn to herd men with cameras on their shoulders, reporters with microphones and recorders out of the way. Dave got a glimpse of Cecil, who stood talking to a blonde young woman from a network news team. Cecil's back was turned. He didn't see Dave pass. Munro drew the car to a halt near the red paramedic van. Next to it lurked the black coroner's wagon, bony Carlyle standing beside this, peering up at the roof of Tiberius Baths, the surrounding lights flickering off his thick glasses. His two helpers, the young Latino, the young Asian, stood talking with attendants from the paramedic vehicle, from the police ambulance, whose rear doors gaped open, waiting.

Jeff Leppard broke from a huddle with the SWAT team, came over to the car, opened the door for Dave to get out.

"I thought you'd come," he said. "Here's the situation. We got a call from the night manager. A man stabbed another man in a hot tub. Manager thinks victim is dead. Lots of screaming and running around, and the manager was able to jump the dude. He had him locked up in a cubicle. He's got a gun, the manager has. All the same, he wants the cops, right?"

"He got them, didn't he," Dave said. "Only why are they all out here?"

"Because when the first car got here, and the officers tried to go in, the perp had made it out of the cubicle and taken the gun away from the manager, and he stood at the top and fired at the officers down the stairs. The door you see is the only way into the whole place. Stairs go up from there to the second floor. And that's it."

"I see a fire escape at the side," Dave said. In the light beams of police cars, five or six officers stood at the foot of the iron fabric in a narrow alley strewn with trash from overflowing dumpsters. "What about the windows?"

"Painted over from inside," Leppard said. "No way to foresee what they'd step into. We voted for the roof. A team is up there now. Skylights are painted over, too, but it's better to drop on him from above. Catch him by surprise."

"Maybe," Dave said. "You going to keep him alive?"

"We want to keep everybody alive." Leppard gazed up at the roof. Shadowy figures moved there. "We don't know how many men might be inside. Phone's off the hook. But if we have to, we'll shoot the perp to save the bystanders."

"He's your only chance to find out who killed Vorse and Prohaska and Bumbry and the rest. Hasn't that been the hangup—no witnesses?"

"No witnesses but you," Leppard said.

"What about the officers he shot at tonight?"

Leppard's laugh was short and grim. "They're still patting themselves all over to be sure they weren't hit. You want him tall and skinny, with long blond hair, right? Hell, they don't even know if he was a human being." He read his

Rolex. "Time's up." He walked back to the SWAT team, took a walkie-talkie from one of them, spoke into it, handed it back. The men around him glanced at the roof, and moved across the street toward the Tiberius Baths, helmets glinting in the fitful lights. They bunched at the door. High above them, metal shrieked, glass shattered, there were thuds, gunshots. The SWAT team burst in at the door, and ran up a narrow stairway. It was brightly lighted. The walls were gold. The carpeting was purple.

Out the window onto the fire escape a figure stumbled. The beam of a spotlight caught and held him. He was short, frail, almost bald. He raised his hands for a second to shield his eyes. Officers started up the fire escape. It clattered under their heels. The man at the top reached behind his back, brought out a handgun, screamed, and fired down at the officers. They fired back. Echoing off the alley walls, the noise was ragged and loud. Dark spots appeared on the grubby sweatshirt of the man at the top. He staggered backward, hit the rail, and toppled over. His body landed on its back in a dumpster, which slowly shed some of its overflow to accommodate him.

13

My name is Leonard Lynn Church. I was born November 13, 1960, in Creon, North Dakota, population 4,500, a farm town, as if there was any other kind in North Dakota. My father was Warren Ross Church, from English people who originally came to Massachusetts in the seventeenth century, and my mother is Elizabeth (Melgard) Church, of Swedish stock from Wisconsin. My musical talent comes from her. She has a nice mezzo voice and plays the piano. It was from her I learned to love classical music. But we fought all the time when she tried to teach me to play, so she hired Victoria Gimbel at five dollars a lesson to teach me. That worked fairly well until I got better at playing than Miss Gimbel—which did not take long. Then I was on my own. I am talking about when I was ten years old. The next year, my sister was seventeen, and went away to college in Northfield, Minnesota, and it was my turn to work in the café.

The café is the "Eat and Run"on Main Street in Creon, and a very popular place, but no one in Creon expects to pay more than a quarter for a cup of coffee or more than two dollars for lunch, or three dollars for supper, and this means the café paid (and I suppose still pays) its owners too poorly to allow them to hire help. After I left Creon, maybe they had to close it down. I hope so. I hated the place. My father cooked, my mother and sister waited on tables, my father kept the books at night.

When I went to work, I knew I wasn't going to be happy, and I dropped and smashed dishes and glassware until keeping me there was simply too expensive. So, except in emergencies, until I got my growth I was allowed to stay home and play the piano and listen to records, which was all I wanted to do at that time. Later on in life, I found I liked sex even more than music, and that was when I left Creon and came to Los Angeles. I will write more about my childhood in Creon later, if I have time.

Because I am dying, I have to get the most important part of my life story told first. I want to write out everything I remember that has ever happened to me in my whole life, but there may not be time. I don't know how long I will have the strength to push this pen, or even hold it in my fingers. I get tired quickly. I have to go out at night and find the ones on my list, and that takes a lot of strength. If I had a tape recorder now, I would just talk all of this into it.

But I don't have a tape recorder anymore. I had an open-reel recorder that cost me two thousand dollars. I had a very good cassette deck. But I had to sell them when they fired me from my programming job at Selwyn & Slaughter. I had worked for them four and a half years! It wasn't the sick leave I had to take to be in the hospital that got me fired. It was the reason I was in the hospital. After I came back to work the second time, Red Selwyn stopped by my desk and asked me quietly to come with him to his office, and told me they had to let me go.

"Why?" I said. "I'm the best and the brightest."

"I know that. But Personnel says you have AIDS. We have to protect the rest of the staff."

"From what? I don't have sex with them. God forbid. Would anyone? Have you looked at them? Mr. Selwyn—that is the only way they could get AIDS from me."

"I know that," he said, "but not everyone believes it. If you don't go, they will. We can't afford that. We also can't afford the group insurance rates we'll be slapped with if you stay. Would that be fair to the others?"

"Keep it our secret," I said. "I've only got two years to live. At most. Be optimistic, why don't you? You could be taking up a

collection to buy flowers for my funeral next week. The doctors
don't know—not for sure."

"The secret's already out." He sat at his desk and didn't look at
me. He put a check into an envelope and held it out to me. "I'm
sorry. I've added two months salary to your regular severance pay.
Good luck." A knife wouldn't have worked with Red Selwyn. I'd
have needed an ice pick to stop his heart. But I wasn't thinking
clearly then. The check came to sixty-four hundred dollars, give
or take, after deductions. I never had so much money in one lump
in my life, and I left stunned not just by being fired suddenly but
by such unexpected wealth.

But the doctors and hospitals soon got it all, didn't they. You
have to be down to seventeen hundred dollars or something before
they'll treat you free. And I couldn't keep a job. If I landed one, it
never lasted. They learned I had AIDS, and I was back on the
street again. Personnel departments ask around. Maybe doctors
and hospitals don't give out the information, but somebody does.
Insurance companies tell other insurance companies. Soon all my
money was gone. So I sold my tape decks, stereo rig, TV, VCR,
records, tapes, books, my furniture, my car, and finally even my
piano. I still cry about that. Then I got thrown out of my apartment.

I am writing this in a garage back of a vacant, boarded-up
house in Venice Beach. I have a sleeping bag, a windbreaker, jeans,
two sweatshirts, underwear, socks, a pair of worn-out Nikes. I
used to dress nicely. I steal Spam, corned beef hash, beans from
the Lucky Supermarket, different times, different shifts. There's
no gas or electricity out here so I have to eat it cold. That's okay.
I'm not really hungry. I only eat to keep me going. This paper and
pen I swiped at Lucky, too. I beg people for change on Ocean Front
Walk, and when I get enough, I take buses to Hollywood. If I have
the money I get a shower at the Y. Then I go on the streets to
find the ones that made me sick so I wound up starving in a filthy
cold garage at the age of twenty-seven. I never had much luck in
my life, otherwise I would be a famous pianist, but I am having
some luck finding the ones I have to kill.

I joke and flirt with them, and not one suspects I'm going to
stick my knife in their heart until I do it. I was nervous the first

109

time that it would be hard, and I was so weak I wondered if I could manage it, but it turned out to be easy, and I don't have butterflies anymore. All that worries me now is that I have fifty-eight names on my list, and I will die before I can get even with them all. I read the obit columns in the Times, and I have found a few names there I could cross off my list because AIDS killed them before I could, but I see others in just the places where I expected to see them, and I will get them. I have been to Junipero Serra, thinking I could kill some in their hospital beds, but that is too dangerous. I mustn't get caught before I finish what I have to do. I wait in the dark places they go to and I used to go to. That's best.

I had better tell about those places and what happens there, because this is the record of my life, and they were important in my life. Everybody should write out their life on paper before they die, otherwise no one will know they lived or what it felt like to be them. When my mother and sister die, and Miss Gimbel, I will be forgotten. For a while, I hung onto tapes I had made of my playing, but somebody ripped them off. They would have shown the world what I could do, that I could make beauty, but now there's nothing. So you will have to take my word for it. All I have left is words. It's raining again. It's too dark. I can't see to write anymore.

The worst thing about being gay is it is risky to try to find somebody to love. Straights have it easy. Any idiot can tell the difference between a man and a woman. You don't have to go circling around some stranger you find attractive, trying to guess if they're gay, scared you'll give yourself away to someone who'll spit on you if you're wrong about them, or will tell everybody you're queer. No wonder gays give up after a while. They settle for sex where it's easy to find. Nobody in the streets, parks, baths, bars has the patience or the courage after a while to risk getting beaten up. They go where they know everybody else is like them. I have to go out now, while the rain has stopped, and cadge quarters for the bus. I had diarrhea for three days, and I couldn't go use my knife. It seems better today. The trick is to drink lots of sugar water with a little salt in it.

Feb. 10—I passed out on the Walk and ended up on County General, very sick, out of my head. I was too weak to leave the hospital for ten whole days, and then I walked out when their backs were turned. I was worried sick somebody would find my stuff here and steal it, or move in themself. But they didn't. I don't need medication yet. Now I have to catch the bus. I kept my quarters. I could take their money after I kill them, but it's bad enough stealing from the supermarket. I am not a thief. I am killing them to make a statement. I want that clear.

Eddie looked so different I hardly knew him when I ran into him in that alley back of the stores on Santa Monica near Croft. He is living with a rich movie director high up in the Monte Verde, and he had great clothes, a nifty haircut, a very expensive watch. He couldn't stop bragging, and I had to interrupt to ask him what time it was, and I was going to miss the last bus to Venice if I stood there any longer, so I stopped his bragging with my knife. He claimed he wasn't sick, but I felt under his armpits, and he had swellings there. Sores in his mouth, too. So it could have been him. I need a watch. I used to own one that cost just as much as his, but I didn't take it. I couldn't wear it. Some policeman might see me looking at it.

Walking to the bus stop, I passed Louie Catlett. We looked at each other, like you do, but it was too bright there from the shop signs for me to kill him. Anyway, I had to rush to catch the bus. That was too bad in another way, because there were darling puppies playing in a pet-shop window, and I felt happy looking at them. It's how you get when you know you're going to die soon. You like to look at anything young, like puppies, kittens, babies. Old people get that way—I've noticed that. It's the same with them. They know they're dying, too. You get old fast with AIDS. It collapses time, a whole life into a few months.

I feel awful. I can't put off getting medication any longer. But I keep having to go farther and farther away to get it now. Because I won't steal money and I can't beg enough. I used to try going to agencies for money, but when you finally get to see somebody, they get all worked up about how you're living and try to put you someplace where you'll get care, and I don't want that because I have my list to take care of, don't I. So I stopped going to agencies. I found a black preacher who gives me cash when he has it, but it's hard for him to get it, too. He's really there to help blacks with AIDS, all right? Because the big AIDS projects think minorities should look after their own. So . . . when I get prescriptions from clinics and hospitals, here is what I do because I don't have any other choice.

I wait and watch the pharmacist make up the prescription through the glass they have, you know, and then I yell there's somebody shoplifting at the front of the store, and they hurry to stop it, and I dodge the counter and grab the pills and run.

But, of course, it means I can never go back. I usually try to get the prescription slip, too. They lay it next to the typewriter when they type up the label, and afterwards they file it, but if I can snatch it when I snatch the medication, then I can use it again, and not have to risk getting hospitalized to get a new one. So yesterday I went over into LA to a drugstore I was never in before.

The reason to get the medication was how awful I felt. I almost let it go too long. I couldn't hardly drag myself out of here. I tried in the morning and kept falling down. It was after three in the afternoon when I finally managed. Raining again by then. I worked my trick on the druggist in Jahrl's across from Chandler Park. As soon as I was in the park I took a pill and laid down on a bench under a tree that kept most of the rain off. It was dark by the time I was able to sit up. The lights came on along the paths. And in maybe half an hour, I headed for my bus stop. And here was Billy Bumbry, looking terrible, black skin stretched over a skeleton. He said he was just out of the hospital, and feeling better, alive again. I led him into the same bushes we had sex in last July, and now he isn't feeling alive anymore, but I am.

Trucks go through Creon, but not much else happens. The movie house tried showing porno stuff, but the churches closed it down, and so that ended even movies there. The porn brought in crowds. The owner could afford to show Disney movies on weekends that way. Everybody in this country wants porn. I read it's an eight-billion-dollar business. But when a pollster *calls up an American and says are you in favor of porn, the American says no, he hates it. He says he hates gays, too, and the stuff they do with each other, but it's just envy and fear the neighbors will think he isn't like them—which is not how he thinks they are.*

I am trying to write about the trucks and what they meant. It is hard for me to keep my thinking straight. I guess my mind is going. I could write the best essays in my high school English classes in Creon. But I keep going off the subject here. The highway is the only exciting thing about Creon, and that is because whiffs of the world blow through on the roaring exhaust of the eighteen-wheelers. I used to lie awake at night listening to them changing gears out on the highway. Was I the only child in Creon that heard the trucks passing in the night and dreamed of going where they go? I doubt it. But I went in a truck, which is not how the rest went, if they ever did. I just had to put out my teenage thumb by the highway. The driver of the rig that helped me climb up beside him liked the bulge in my pants. That was why he stopped. I wish he'd been going east instead of west. If I'd gone to New York, I might have become a famous pianist. You can't do that in LA.

It's easy to collect thrown-away newspaper along the Walk, and I read about the stabbings each morning after they happen. An old queen in a hotdog stand on the pier at Santa Monica gave me hot coffee this morning, and a donut. I don't know where he came from, but if he keeps giving food away he won't last long. He gave me two dollars out of the cash register, too. "You look so sick," he said. "God, I was lucky to get all that sex stuff behind me before AIDS came along." He leaned across the counter and whispered to me, bad teeth, bad breath, red nose, "Do you know, I never even had clap? I mean, I had sex everyplace, darling, anyplace, with anybody, and I never even got clap. Your generation—they really ran out of luck." If I find him out at night, I'll kill him, too. Under the pier.

All right, now, get yourself together. What you are trying to write here is that Blackie Rose's body was never found. They don't know he's dead. They found Frank Prohaska. He was so neat, like a store-window dummy, not a hair out of place. But his ears stuck out. That was what was cute about him. They found Art Lopez. He was blind. I could tell. "Who's that?" he said. "Lynn Church," I said, so he would know. "This is for what you did to me." They found him and Sean and Frank and Billy and Eddie. They never found Blackie. Maybe I should write and tell them where he is up there off Mulholland. I had to lie down beside him afterwards to rest. It was the first time I ever laid outdoors in the dark with a dead man.

So when the papers say I have killed five, they are wrong. I have killed six. Then today the paper says a man named Dodge was stabbed and it was my work. He was young like the rest, and he had AIDS. At first I thought I was losing my memory. They told me in the hospital my brain is shrinking. That happens with AIDS. So I got out my list, but didn't find any Drew Dodge on it. I didn't think so. Anyway, last night it was raining, and I didn't go out. The next time it doesn't rain, I will go to the Tiberius Baths. I am coughing too much. Sometimes I cough so hard, I pass out. I can't risk the rain.

I need a fat suit to disguise myself, don't I? I am so thin now, anybody can tell I'm dying. The old auntie at the hotdog stand knew right off. I mean, if you're male and young, then what's killing you these days is AIDS, isn't it? They may not let me in at Tiberius. But so much happened to me there, so many. There's the bars, too. The Beejay. I was not born to die this way. I was given a perfect body by God. I was never once sick a day in my whole life. Look what they have done to me. I will find one of them when I go to the Tiberius Baths. I don't know who it will be. He doesn't know, either. We will both get a surprise, won't we?

14

In Leppard's office, with its metal desk and file cabinets, the rattle of rain on the vertical metal slats outside the windows made a gentle background for Leppard's ungentle speech. "He'll never accept it, and you know that. Sure, we can cut out the part about how Church didn't kill Dodge. Hell, we can suppress the whole damn thing." He lifted and let fall back to the desk Leonard Lynn Church's pitiful try at writing out his life story in ballpoint ink on twenty-one pages of blue-lined school notebook paper. "The press and TV will call us dirty names, but it won't last forever."

"What will last forever," Dave said, "is police officers guarding me around the clock, following me wherever I go. I appreciate the thought, but—"

"The kid is going to keep trying to kill you," Leppard said. "He won't believe for a minute we've settled on Church as the one who stabbed Dodge and attacked you. We released his description, Dave. Remember?"

"I missed that. In the hospital. It was a mistake."

"We wanted the public's help," Leppard said. "We had every reason to think he was the one."

"Then you shouldn't have let Church's picture out."

"You saw that street," Leppard said. "Every reporter in town, including your friend Harris. Cameras had Church on film the minute he came out that window. The alley was all lit up. Telephoto lenses. What the hell could I do? They had a clear sight line from the top of their trucks."

"Right." Dave nodded. "Sorry." He sighed, rose, went for his trenchcoat by the office door. "Why don't we leave it this way—if he doesn't take a crack at me in the next few days, you call your people off."

Leppard got to his feet back of the desk, stretched, yawned. "I've got a better idea. Take a vacation. You ever been to the Virgin Islands? Beautiful. And cheap this time of year."

"No doubt." Dave had shed the sling. If he was careful not to reach too far or too high, his shoulder gave him almost no pain. Flapping into the trenchcoat involved some discomfort, but he only winced a little. He put on the Irish hat, damp on the outside, dry within, the wool fat still in the yarn. He took hold of the doorknob. "But I want to be here when you catch Baby," he said. He frowned again at the pages on the desk. "It doesn't explain much, really, does it? The thought must have gone through the heads of hundreds of youngsters dying of AIDS like Church that the men they'd had sex with were to blame. But only he went around stabbing them to death."

"Yeah, well," Leppard said with a sour smile, "it doesn't give the reason he left Creon, North Dakota, very suddenly one hot September night in 1976, either, does it?"

"He didn't like working in the café," Dave said.

"He didn't like it so much," Leppard said, "that after closing time that night, he picked up a butcher knife in the kitchen and stabbed his father in the chest, and left him for dead on the greasy linoleum."

"He didn't die," Dave said. "You told me you talked to him long distance, that he's coming to pick up the body and take it back to Dakota for burial."

"He didn't die," Leppard said. "Little Leonard had things to learn about stabbing people in those days. He got better at it later, right?"

"It was his way of solving problems," Dave said.

"You think about going down there to the Caribbean," Leppard said. "White beaches, clear blue ocean, warm tropic sun. And best of all, the kid can't follow you there. Jet travel is expensive. And he wears rags—didn't you say he wears rags?"

"He had money for a gun," Dave said, and left.

The car that followed him up Laurel Canyon was a black-and-white. It parked half in the ditch, water running fast and hub deep around its tires. The idea was to spook the kid, not catch him. Tonight they'd assign an unmarked car again and hope he'd appear with murder on his mind. Dave tapped the Jaguar's horn and lifted a hand to the uniforms inside the car, as he swung into his bricked and puddled yard. The young officer behind the wheel of the black-and-white gave him a poker-faced nod. Dave parked the Jaguar, left the key in the ignition, got out, made a conspicuous gesture of looking at his watch, then walked out to the patrol car. The driver rolled the window down.

"My mechanic will be coming to pick up my car," Dave told him. "Any time now. Don't worry about it."

"Thanks for telling us," the youngster said.

"Thanks for being here," Dave said.

Inside the rear building, which smelled, as it always did in wet weather, of the horses that had been stabled in it long ago, he didn't take off hat or trenchcoat. He sat at the desk and pushed buttons on the telephone. The number was Kevin Nakamura's at his service station down the canyon. It took a minute to get past the woman who answered. It took less to tell Nakamura what he wanted.

He moved to the bar under the overhang of the new sleeping loft, found a squat bottle, sloshed brandy into a snifter. He lit a cigarette. Brandy was less than it could be without smoke to go with it. He leaned on the bar, listened to the rain patter on the shingles high overhead, and savored the brandy and smoke. He took his time. But when he heard Nakamura's wrecker arrive and depart out front, the door of the Jaguar slam, its engine rumble to life, he snuffed his cigarette, finished the brandy, walked briskly down the room and outside, shutting the door behind him.

Standing in the rain, he studied the steep hillside that rose back of his place. It was thick with undergrowth, dark with dripping trees. He had never climbed it. It would be nice if he were in better shape now that he had to, but life wasn't like that. He ducked under the winter-bare vine on its arbor that backed the courtyard, hitched his way up the stony retaining wall and, using his good right arm to push aside the brittle branches of wet wild privet, began to climb, crouching, dodging, feet slipping on matted leaves and mud. He stumbled more than once, grubbying his hands, sending stabs of pain into his shoulder, soiling the knees of his trousers. But he made it to the top, another loop of Horseshoe Canyon Trail, where Nakamura waited in the Jaguar.

Grinning, the mechanic reached across and opened the passenger door for Dave. "I always liked playing cops and robbers," he said.

"Be devious." Dave got in and shut the door. "Take Faro down to Mesquite. That way they won't see us. I'll drop you at your place and take it alone from there."

"Aw," Nakamura said. "I'm disappointed."

The trees had lost their yellow blossoms. The rains and winds had stripped them. Street sweepers had cleared them from the gutters. He parked and locked the Jaguar about where Drew Dodge had left his car on the night he died. Dave climbed a set of steps like those that led to Carmen Lopez's apartment across the street. The door he wanted today was the first of the row of brass-numbered doors along the outside gallery. By this one, glass wind chimes hung tinkling from the roof overhang that kept the rain off Dave while he waited for the door to open.

Sonia White was surely eighty, maybe older, skinny, stringy, but weirdly girlish. She didn't work at this—her withered face was innocent of makeup, her hair was cropped, the color of oatmeal. What appeared to be a lens, rectangular, framed in sturdy black plastic, almost like a welder's mask, was fastened around her head with a black strap. She had hinged it up above her large, bright hazel eyes so she could look at Dave. She did this with the brisk attentiveness of a bird.

"Yes?" Her voice was chirpy. "How can I help you?"

"By talking to me"—Dave held out his investigator's license to her—"about the boy you saw hanging around on the night of the murder across the street."

She jerked a little with surprise. "Ah, indeed? I thought that was all over. They caught the killer. Night before last. I saw it on the news. Dreadful. So sad."

"But he wasn't the boy you saw," Dave said. "The boy you saw was tall and thin and had long blond hair."

"True." She frowned and worried that fact for a second, then shivered and brought Dave into focus again. "Oh, do come inside. It's cold, isn't it? What wretched weather we're having." She backed into the room, clutching a slate-blue jacket closed at her throat with spidery, ink-stained fingers. She hurriedly shut the door. Dave remembered—it was a Chairman Mao jacket. "Well, then," she said, dismissively, "my boy had nothing to do with it, did he? After all, I didn't see him stab that man, Dodge, in the garage across the street. I only saw him loitering."

The room smelled strongly of incense. The same time-server had laid out this apartment as had laid out Carmen Lopez's. The plan was identical. But this was no living room, it was a workroom. It held three long tables on tubular metal legs, the Formica tops bound with metal strips. The tables were piled with books, papers, scrolls. Strong lights bent over them on armatures, like fishing herons. Many of the books were large, old, calf-bound. Ceiling-high shelves lined the walls, crowded with books. A cat slept curled up on an old manual typewriter in a corner. Age-stained cardboard cartons overflowed with handwritten pages on the shelf between the living room and kitchenette.

"What about hot tea?" she said, and hurried off in her floppy Mao trousers, calling back, "It keeps me going, I'll tell you. I don't know where I'd be without hot tea. The kettle's always on here. Now, you kitties, please make room." Dave heard thumps and meows of protest. "They lie on the stove, as near to the hot water as they can get." She laughed briefly. "I love them, but they're not always as considerate of others as they might be. Yes, pretty things. Now, then, be careful. You'll knock the pot right out of my hand." China rattled.

"Can I help?" Dave said.

"It's all right," she fluted. "I'm used to it." In a moment, she came in breathless, bearing a Chinese-patterned cup on its saucer in each hand. "Though I do imagine sometimes that they realize I'm getting frail, and they push their luck a little more each day." She laughed again and set the cups down on a bare corner of the nearest table. She looked around. "Let's see. A place to sit." She took a stack of old wooden in-out boxes off a straight wooden chair, gave Dave a smile of bright false teeth. "There, now." She turned and wheeled a secretary's chair up close. "Do sit down." Dave sat. Cats came and jumped up on the table to sniff at the steam from the cups, eyes half closed, noses wiggling. The steam was aromatic. "It's China tea. I'm thankful to Mr. Nixon. Whatever his faults, he let me have my China tea again."

Dave took the fragile cup up and touched the hot tea to his mouth. "So that's what they mean by tea," he said.

"Yes," she laughed, "not made from twigs, is it?"

"Wonderful," he said, set down the cup, dug out his reading glasses, and peered at the work on the table under the hard light. "Chinese," he said. "What are you working on, may I ask?"

"I'd be devastated if you didn't." She laughed at herself again, but it was probably the truth. "A long, long novel, variously called *The Dream of the Red Chamber, The Story of the Stone*, and *The Twelve Beauties of Jin Ling.* Written by one Tsao Shwe Chin, sometime around 1765."

"You're translating it," Dave said.

"I have been, it seems, for a lifetime." She sighed, pushed at the papers in front of her with those veined and bony hands of hers. "It's taken altogether too long. The whole thing's been published lately by translators in England—1980, I think it was. Five volumes." She picked up her cup, gave him a brave smile, said, "But I press on. I've found innumerable bits to quarrel with their version." She sipped some tea, clicked the cup back in its saucer. "As any Chinese translator would, of course. The written or printed characters can be enormously complicated, you see, and the eye is sometimes fooled." She pulled a large book to her, opened it, laid a finger on a character. Dave peered. She said, "Here, for example—inside all of these strokes lurk what are called radicals—simple symbols for ordinary concepts, bamboo, house, man, horse, and so forth. And to find the correct meaning of this particular ideogram, one must determine which is the operative radical." She dodged a glance at him, and closed the book. "Oh, dear, I'll bore you silly. Never mind. At least my version will be in American English. It seems wrong to me somehow for those dear little Chinese servant girls to speak like London scullery maids on public television."

"What made you look outside that night?" Dave said.

"What? Oh, dear—I don't know. Resting my eyes, I suppose." She touched the lens contraption on her head. Then she laughed and put her hands on her back. "Or my poor, aching sacroiliac. I get absorbed and sit too long, and how it aches when I remember." She blinked to herself, drank a little more tea. "And then I sometimes open the

door when it rains. I love the freshness of the washed air."
She frowned, held up a hand. "Wait. I remember. So many
car doors closing on this ordinarily quiet street." She
nodded firmly. "That was it. I went to have a look."

"And where was the boy, exactly?"

"I told the police." She lifted a cat down onto her lap
from the table. "But perhaps they didn't tell you."

"Not in detail," Dave said.

"He drove up the street, just as I stepped out on the gallery."
She frowned to herself and spoke slowly. She stroked the
cat. It purred. "He parked about two doors along. It was a
rackety old car, some dark color. He got out of it straight
away, and turned to look back. I heard still another car door
slam, just out in front here. And I saw the man whose name
I later learned was Dodge, poor fellow, cut at an angle across
the street toward the building opposite this one. I have an
impression, actually, of two men, Dodge and someone
shorter, but the light was poor. They exchanged words, but
I couldn't make them out. Anyway, the tall blond boy began
to run towards them. Then the wind blew rain into my face,
and I came back inside." She said to the cat, "Oh, what a
lovely purr, Bao-Chai."

"The boy and Dodge didn't quarrel?"

"The police asked me that, too. I didn't hear them." She
set the cat on the floor, stood, reached for his cup.

"I'd better go." Dave pushed his glasses away, rose, and
began buttoning his trenchcoat. "You've plainly got a lot
of work ahead. I'd feel guilty keeping you from it."

Her large, clear eyes said she'd rather he stayed—the
work would always be here. But she resignedly set her cup
down, and followed him to the door. She watched him put
on the tweed hat. When he pulled open the door, she filled
her lungs gratefully with the damp air. He stepped outside,
and she said, "Something slipped my mind when the police
were here. I wonder if it meant anything, if I ought to have
told them."

"What was it?" Dave said.

"A noise. Startling in the quiet. I'd only just got back in my chair, adjusted my reading glass, and found my place in the text, when there was this loud pop."

Dave tilted his head. "A gunshot?"

"Well, of course, there was violence over there, but I didn't know that then, did I? I thought it was a backfire. You see, when Mr. Dodge used to come, he and the boy across the street often rode out on motorcycles at night. They kept the machines garaged over there. And sometimes they were noisy. Well, I'd seen Mr. Dodge arrive, so that was my assumption, a backfire." She frowned. "Was it a gunshot? It was a knife that killed him."

"That's right," Dave said. "Thank you. May I trouble you just a minute more? I'd like to use your phone."

She was delighted. He rang the coroner's office and got Carlyle on the line. "Can you examine Dodge's hands for gunpowder?" he asked. But it was too late. Dodge's body had been released to his family for burial.

15

THE HOUSE LOOKED from the coast road much as when he'd last seen it—raw boards, tall reaches of glass, jutting beams, roof angles, decks. A long bridge of planks crossed the dunes to the house. The bridge looked sturdy, held together by big, rust-bleeding bolts, but it rumbled and shook under the weight of the Jaguar. He parked on a stretch of deck beside garages attached to the house, and got out into a mist of rain, the smell of ocean, the heavy thud of surf. He stood gazing at the surf for a moment, trying to put a name to its color. Rose gray? The color of the sand it was churning up. White foam laid lace on the glassy sand, reaching clear up under the house. Over the sharp roofs, ragged clouds hung, smudged grays and blacks. He poked a bellpush under a metal tag, THOMAS OWENS, AIA. When he'd come here first, dogs had barked at him from inside, clawed the door.

"What happened to the dogs?" he asked Tom Owens.

"It's been twelve years." The man with the knobby face and odd yellow eyes smiled. "They're dead, Dave. Old age. Trudy took one, Gail the other." He meant the niece he'd raised, and her mother, his sister. "But they're gone now. Barney was killed that night, you know."

Dave knew. To gain entrance to the house, Owens's would-be killer had shot Barney, a big, quiet fellow, fawn-colored, with a black saddle marking, droopy ears, and yellow eyes like his master's. The other dogs were small, and had run frightened out onto the dunes in the dark. "I remember," Dave said, and let Owens help him off with his coat. He pushed the hat into a pocket. Owens hung the coat in a shallow closet that breathed out cedar when he closed the door. Dave said, "Did Trudy marry that boy Dimond?"

"Dimond?" Owens's brow wrinkled as he searched his memory. "Oh, right. The one devoted to tape recording every sound in nature." Owens's short laugh was ironical. "And some not quite so natural."

"That one," Dave said, and walked down into the vast main room, where he stood gazing again at the stormy blue-black abstract painting that stretched along the wall opposite the windows that looked out on the beach. The room lofted high, with steep angles, tall shafts. It was the best-looking room he knew. "I guess not, right?"

"The son of Gail's psychoanalyst. The one Gail went to for help. It came to that. You were the catalyst, did you know? You made her see"—Owens grew aware of Dave watching him closely, poker-faced—"made us both see our attachment to each other was unhealthy. Misplaced mutual dependency. Destroying both of us."

"That doesn't sound like me," Dave said. "I'm given to short words when I can find them."

"In the form of questions, right, that's true." Owens passed him, led the way down the room, past groupings of unpainted wicker furniture with sailcloth cushions, and into a high-reaching hallway where Dave remembered standing tense that heart-pounding night while beyond this door right here the man who'd come to kill Owens whined his twisted reasons, if they could be called that. "No, the words are the analyst's." Owens opened the door. "But you were the diagnostician." The room beyond the door had served as a hospital room that long-ago time. Owens had lain here with both legs in casts. It was easier to nurse him downstairs. Now the room was back to its original use. It was a drafting office, with stretches of beautiful tilted white pine tables, glinting drawing instruments, scrolls of plans and blueprints, a pair of glossy computers. Owens opened a gray metal storage cabinet, bottles and glasses shelved inside. "A drink before lunch?" he said, and with a smile, "It's good having you here again. It's been too long."

"I agree. I love this house. I don't know why I've never been back. I regret the occasion. It shouldn't have taken a death to bring me. Malt whisky, thanks." He had spotted Glenfiddich in the cabinet. He watched Owens pour into roomy glasses. "So, Trudy married the psychoanalyst. What about Gail? She was the one who needed a man to look after in place of her brother."

"You remember Elmo Sands, the contractor?" Owens put a glass into Dave's hand. "The one who built this place for me?" Dave nodded, and Owens said, "He lost his wife to cancer. Gail married him. He's nothing like me—maybe that's why they're happy together." He perched on a draftsman's stool.

Dave sat at one of the computer desks and asked, "Would Sands by any chance be the contractor on the Rancho Vientos shopping mall?"

Owens blinked. "Matter of fact, yes. My suggestion."

"Right. I want to talk to him. I want to talk to everybody involved with Drew Dodge."

"The funeral's tomorrow morning," Owens said. "I expect most of them will be there. Drew was a winning kid." Owens tasted his whisky. "Everybody loved him."

"Not quite everybody," Dave said. "If it's all right with you, I'll get a motel room down the road, and we can go to the funeral together."

"Stay here," Owens said. "There are plenty of guest rooms. Call Cecil. Get him to come down here, too."

Dave shook his head. "He works at night. And I'd put you in danger, staying here." He didn't answer Owens's puzzled look. He worked on the whisky, and said, "You understand, Dodge's wasn't one of the serial killings. It only looked that way. Somebody else stabbed him."

"The blackmailer didn't get what he wanted?" Owens said. "Drew couldn't come up with the money, time ran out, and he killed him?" Owens cocked his head, an eyebrow raised. "Am I guessing right?"

"Guesses don't often help," Dave said. "Was the blackmailer a tall, skinny kid around twenty, with long blond hair held back by a narrow bandana headband? Ragged jeans, tanktop, dirty tennis shoes?"

Owens shook his head, swallowed whisky. "Drew didn't describe him. Is that what he looked like?"

"A witness saw him on the street where Dodge was killed on the night he was killed. I saw him myself, later."

Owens frowned. "Was he the one who jumped you, the one who cut your shoulder?"

Dave nodded. "And you figure Dodge had had sexual relations with him, and he was threatening to expose him?"

"Why else come to me?" Owens said. "Drew had been here, met Larry, seen what we were to each other. That night, he apologized for bothering me, but I was the only one he could turn to. Didn't that mean because we were both gay?"

"Had he ever told you he was gay?"

Owens's laugh was short and wry. "I see where you're coming from. No, he hadn't. I assumed he knew I knew."

"Why didn't he pay, and get it over with?"

"He didn't have the money. He'd been in the hospital, a long stay, with pneumonia. He was broke, needed time to get back on his feet. And this bastard wanted big bucks. Drew grabbed at your card. He was scared."

"What scares us isn't necessarily what kills us." Dave got to his feet. "And blackmail's a lousy motive for murder. You can't get money from a dead man." He studied glassed drawings on the wall. Only the shapes of the buildings were familiar, not the lawns, walks, landscaping. "Somebody else is scared now—the kid who tried to kill me. Which is why I won't stay here tonight." Lettering below the drawings read: SHOPPING MALL, RANCHO VIENTOS, 1987. "Handsome," Dave said.

"There'll be more trees," Owens said. "The city council is sore about the oaks we took down. They're making us replace them with twice the number."

Dave said, "So—Larry hung on, did he? You're still together? I didn't know for sure. You haven't talked about him, and I didn't like to ask. You never know when you're going to give pain with that question."

"We're together," Owens said. "I never thought I'd be so lucky, but it happened, and it's wonderful. He tried to learn drafting so he could work with me." Owens gave a sorry laugh and shook his head. "The math sank him. But he's turned into a pretty fair artist—commercial, freelance. It lets him earn his own money, and that's important to him. And he can work at home. And that's more important to him, not ever to have to leave here." Owens gestured to indicate ocean, rocks, dunes, the house. "The only arguments we have are when I ask him to go out with me—to a restaurant, the music center, the museum. He'd rather stay home. Worse than that, he'd rather I stayed home, never went anyplace."

"That's why he never came with you to my house," Dave said. "Well, there had to be something." Through a rainy window, he watched breakers crash on rocks for a moment. "The interpretation you put on Dodge's visit—could it have got in the way of your remembering anything he said or did?"

"I suppose, but I don't think so. It's hard to forget opening the door at midnight to a man you only know in a business way, and hardly recognize, disheveled, soaked with rain, at his wit's end, begging for your help."

"I'm told the shopping mall is in deep trouble. He didn't mention that?"

"Elmo Sands keeps mentioning it. But, no, Drew didn't talk about it. He'd have known how to handle that, young Drew would. Extortion he didn't know how to handle."

Dave mused, working on his drink. "You didn't advise him to buy a gun?"

"Good God, no." Owens peered at Dave. "What made you think that? I told you—I gave him your card. I had a time finding it. Rummaged it out of a drawer in here, at last. Couldn't remember where the hell I'd put it. I only parted with it because he seemed to need you as badly as I once did. May I have another?"

Dave took out his wallet, slid a card from it, passed the card to Owens. To reach across the table made his shoulder hurt. "But don't get into trouble." He pushed the wallet away. "I'm retiring."

Owens stared. "You're joking."

"No, I'm fed up with hospitals. The world is getting meaner by the week. And I'm not quick enough anymore." Dave told him about the shooting at Haven House. "I don't want to die on some rainy sidewalk. I want to die in bed. With Cecil holding on to me."

"How is he?" Owens said. "I missed him at the hospital."

"He's living with a young lady, these days," Dave said. "I'm waiting for the situation to resolve itself. It's taking longer than I like. Longer than I've got to spare for it." The subject troubled him, and he lit a cigarette. "Sorry." He held the cigarette up. "Is this all right?"

"With fifty million Americans," Owens said. "It's a death-wish thing, you know. Slow suicide."

Dave laughed. "A simple yes or no will do."

"Yes, of course," Owens said. And frowned, remembering. "I just can't bring this skinny twenty-year-old kid of yours into true with what Drew said. He said the blackmailer came from long ago and far away. Wouldn't that mean he'd have to be older, Drew's contemporary? He said, "I thought I'd left all that behind forever. I wasn't even the same person then." What do you suppose that meant?"

"Where did he hail from?" Dave said.

"I don't know." Owens found on the drawing table a high-sided blue glass dish of pushpins and paper clips. He emptied these into a drawer, and handed the dish to Dave for an ashtray. "I met with him pretty often while I was designing the buildings, but those were work sessions. A few times socially, mostly at parties. We never had an intimate conversation."

"Not till the night before he was killed."

"Not till then. And then he was holding back a lot."

"Oh? What made you think that?"

"The way he couldn't sit still, kept jumping up and pacing. He wanted to tell me all about it. I could sense that, the whole story wanting to be told. But he couldn't work up his nerve."

"Which is why you suggested me," Dave said.

"He jumped at that. I could see the relief in his face. You'd be a stranger, right? He could tell you on a professional basis, no fear of a friend's disapproval—if that's what I was, a friend. No fear it might go farther—back to his wife, say. Or his business associates."

"Did he tell you he had AIDS?"

Owens bleakly shook his head. "Not that, either."

"He never mentioned his childhood to you—South, Midwest, New England? Farm, city? Did he name a college?"

Owens moved his bony shoulders. "I'm sorry. If he did, I don't remember. He seemed—well, so rooted in California. It never occurred to me he might come from someplace else. Funny. Most of us do, don't we? Don't you?"

Dave laughed, shook his head. "Pasadena," he said.

Larry Johns appeared in the doorway, hair bleached by the sun, skin toasted by the sun, eyes bright blue. He was no longer a willowy boy. He'd thickened. His voice had got deeper. Nor was he pretty anymore. Still, his face had a pleasant, open look to it. "Hi, Mr. Brandstetter." He came in and held out his hand. He brought a tang of the kitchen with him, onions, cheeses, peppers. Dave shook the hand. Johns said, "Nice to see you again. Been catching a lot of killers lately?"

"Not the one I want," Dave said. "You look fine."

"I had long hair and a moustache when we met." Johns laughed. "How long has it been? Ten years, right?"

"Tom says twelve," Dave said.

Johns looked at Owens. "Lunch will be ready in twenty minutes. I've got time to have a drink with you."

"Well planned." Owens smiled, gave him a quick hug and kiss, got off the stool, took Dave's glass to the cabinet with his own, and this time made three drinks. Dave lit another cigarette. He missed Cecil.

Seated at a shelf facing rainy glass that looked out on the ocean from high up in the house, they ate the guacamole, enchiladas, refritos Larry had cooked, washing them down with Mexican beer. Dave liked this tower room, shelves of books, tapes, records. An armatured lamp bent over a drawing table. Pinned to the plank walls were nice loose watercolors of the dunes, the sharp rocks in the surf, the house. A pine cabinet held art supplies, another one games. They rotated bouts of chess, played to a time clock. Dave left at four.

But when he rumbled the Jaguar out onto the rock-strewn coast road, an unmarked police car waited for him. He pulled up beside it, tapped his horn, triggered a switch to lower the window on the passenger side. The leathery Dugan was in the car, slouched down behind the wheel, hat tilted forward over his eyes. But not asleep. He sat straight, pushed the hat back, winced at Dave, rolled-down his window.

Dave said, "I'll sleep here tonight. Tomorrow morning I'll drive to Drew Dodge's funeral in Rancho Vientos."

"Sure you will," Dugan said.

"Can I bring you coffee from the house? A sandwich?"

"I'm okay." Dugan held up a thermos bottle for a second. "What you could do for me is go home and stay there."

"You don't enjoy the beach?" Dave said.

Dugan gave a sour snort, rolled up his window, pulled the hat over his eyes, and slouched behind the wheel again.

16

THE STORM BLEW on inland overnight. The morning sky was the scrubbed shiny blue of Dutch tiles. The hills to the right of the coast road were napped in fresh spring green. All this corner of the continent needed was a little rain, and the grass sprang up. To the left, the breakers crashed, foam ran up the dark, sleek sand. Trailers and campers parked along that sand. Kids and dogs ran around them. A young couple unhitched bicycles from racks. Wind flapped the hat brims of an old couple fishing from canvas chairs.

After an hour, Dave cut back through the hills, and the valley he dropped down into was also green in the morning light. Quiet still held the main street of Rancho Vientos, dew sparkling on the roofs of a few cars at the curbs. Passing the hardware store, Dave wondered if Drew Dodge had bought a handgun there. Tom Owens's black BMW didn't turn off toward the residential section in the hills, but led Dave on out the highway, northwestward. The church stood in a wide meadow. Newly built to an old design. Frame. Steeple. Gray with white trim.

A blacktop parking area lay to the east of the building, the white bias lines painted on it still fresh, the shrubs and trees surrounding it still new, fragile. Owens parked. Dave put the Jaguar into the slot beside the BMW. A detective with a moustache parked an unmarked LAPD car near the lot entrance. And stayed seated in the car, steadfastly looking at nothing. Dave and Owens got out into the fresh country morning air. Their car doors closing sounded noisy in the quiet. Far off a meadowlark sang. Crows cawed. Dave read his watch, and looked a question at Owens.

"Maybe I got the time wrong," Owens said.

Dave doubted it, but he walked to the rear of the church. In cold shadow there stood a black stretch limousine and a hearse with curtained windows, its rear door open, a frame on rollers projecting slightly, waiting to receive a coffin. A third car was parked back here, a car he'd last seen covered with twigs, leaves, yellow blossoms on the street in LA where Art Lopez used to live. It was a sand-color late-model Mercedes four-door, the Dodge family automobile. Luggage was in the rear seat, a stuffed panda, a plastic robot. Organ music reached Dave. He read his watch and touched Owens's arm.

"You weren't wrong about the time," he said. "We'd better go inside."

Owens made a face. "I hate these things, under the best of circumstances." Tense and unhappy, he walked beside Dave. He stopped, looked around at the empty parking lot, looked at Dave. "It's because he was gay, right? Because he had AIDS. Jesus, the man had five hundred friends. Now look."

"Forget it," Dave said. "It can't hurt him now."

"Who's the Mexican?" Owens nodded at the police car. "What's he doing here? I never saw him before."

"He's a police officer. He's guarding me." Dave eyed the man for a minute, and chewed his lower lip. Then he took Owens's elbow. "Come on, let's get inside." The damp perfume of cut flowers hung in the church vestibule. Dave halted there, took off his hat, set it on Owens's head, and painfully shed his trenchcoat. "I need your help. Put this on."

Owens blinked bewilderment, but he did as Dave asked. "The keys to my car are in the right-hand pocket."

Owens felt the pocket, nodded, straightened the hat.

"Now, what I want you to do is go through the chancel and out the back door of the church, get into my car, and drive it away. Not toward town. North. Understand?"

"But the funeral—" Owens began.

"You can come back for that. All I need is five minutes with my watchdog out of the way. I'll take your car. Give me the keys. Or don't you want to do it?"

"Did you save my life?" Owens put the BMW keys in Dave's hand. "Do you think I've forgotten?"

Owens opened the door into the chapel. Dave caught the door, stepped after him into a wash of organ music, sat in a rear pew. Kathy Dodge, Gerda Nilson, and two children sat in the front pew. No one else was here. In a small town to live respectably was not enough—you had to die respectably, and Dodge's respectability had ended with his life, when his secrets were no longer secret. That was why nobody with a choice was here. Who was the dead man, anyway? No one Rancho Vientos had known. Tom Owens walked down the aisle, paused and bent to murmur a few words to Kathy Dodge, then crossed the chancel to a rear door, stepped out, and closed the door quietly behind him.

Dave sat staring at the casket on its trestle. Flowers blanketed the casket. Only one other floral piece stood by, gladioli in a white wicker basket, probably from Owens. Dave scowled to himself. Secrets? Not all of them were out. What was the third, the one Dodge had been on his way to tell Dave when death intervened? Did others besides the long-haired skinny boy who kept raging after Dave know that one? Was the boy acting on his own? Or was someone paying him?

The engine of the Jaguar rumbled to life outside. Dave waited, heart beating fast. Then a second engine started, and he smiled to himself. With a finger, he pushed back a jacket cuff, and watched the sweep hand of his watch tick past all the numbers. A gray-haired man in a turned-around collar and a black suit came out the door Owens had left by. A prayer book was in the man's hand. He spread the book open on a lectern, looked at Kathy Dodge, Gerda Nilson, and the children, raised his eyes and looked at Dave. Dave got up and left the church.

The curved street lay quiet in the morning sunlight. The sprawling, low-slung houses might have been vacant under their long ramps of shake roofing. Here and there, automatic sprinkler systems sprayed lawns and flower beds as if it hadn't rained for weeks. A square little Postal Service jeep, white with blue and red trim, puttered toward him, stopping at each curbside mailbox. There was no other traffic. If people drove to work here, if they drove their kids to school, that was finished for today.

He parked Owens's BMW on the street, and crunched up the white gravel of the drive. He made his way alongside the Dodge house to the rear. A tall gate in a grapestake fence let him into a spacious backyard, where an oval swimming pool mirrored the blue of the sky. Flowering shrubs and vines, clumps of quick-growing trees edged the yard. Wooden lawn furniture faced a brick barbecue in a far corner. A screened lanai had been added to the back of the house. Its aluminum door opened for him. He crossed the lanai among glass-topped tables and directors' chairs, tried the house back door, found it unlocked, and stepped inside.

He passed a washer and dryer, storage cupboards that gave off smells of soap, disinfectants, rubber gloves. A door stood open on a small bathroom—toilet, basin, shower. Then he was in the kitchen, a broad room with rough, crooked beams, rustic cupboards, hanging copper-bottomed pans. Dishes lay in the sink. The air smelled of the morning's coffee and of cinnamon. A serving window showed him a generous dining room. He wanted the den. If Dodge picked and chose the paperwork he let Judith Ober handle for him, then maybe the rest came home here.

Dave opened doors on two neat guest bedrooms before he found the den. It had a brick fireplace, a handful of shiny sports trophies on the mantel. The furniture was oak, imitation nineteenth-century American, rolltop desk, file cabinet, swivel chair, a small table that held a gleaming white late-model typewriter. Leather wing chairs faced the fireplace, a table between them holding a brass student lamp with a green glass shade. A tufted easy chair in rich brown leather dozed in a corner.

Dust lay on everything. No one had been in here for days. Which meant Leppard hadn't bothered. Not yet. Dave was getting first crack. At what? He opened a file drawer and wished he had more time. Funerals and graveside ceremonies didn't take long. He'd have to hurry. He drew back curtains on leaded windows, put on his reading glasses, and went to work. He skimmed files of letters, making mental notes of names and dates. Two letters startled him, and he folded them, tucked them into an inside jacket pocket. Other files held newspaper clippings. Most dealt with squabbles between the city council and land developers, Drew Dodge among them, with angry licks from private householders against both sides. One clipping stopped him. It noticed an LA television talk show on which Drew Dodge appeared only days before his death. Dave pocketed this, too. He put back the contents of drawer one, shut the drawer, opened drawer two, transferred its contents to the desk, shuffled through it, scowling. He read his watch and began to sweat. Time was running out.

What he had here were canceled checks, back statements, mortgage and tax payment receipts, and stacks of bills, mostly unpaid. Apart from a receipt for the purchase of a Browning 9mm pistol at a Santa Barbara gun shop dated the day after the television show, the jumble told him little he didn't already know.

He dumped it back into drawer two, and rifled drawer three. Sitting down in the twanging swivel chair to sort this out, he realized his head ached. From tension, or eyestrain? He switched on a desk lamp. And out of the corner of his eye saw a square of paper that had fallen to the rug. He leaned, stretched, picked it up. Rain-wrinkled. Handwritten. Gritty. He began to smooth it out in the light of the lamp.

And heard someone pass outside. Breathing. Footfalls. He poked the letter into the side pocket of his jacket, swept up the piles of stuff from the desk, returned them to the third drawer. The lanai screen door rattled. Dave pushed the file drawer shut. The door from the lanai closed. Dave drew the window curtains, switched off the desk lamp, left the den for the living room. The curtains here were closed so he doubted he could be seen by the short, stout man who came down the hallway past the guest room doors and, plainly knowing right where it was, went into the den. The floor of the hallway was polished broad hardwood boards, but the soles of Dave's shoes were soft and he moved to the den door soundlessly and put his ear to it.

A file drawer opened. Papers rustled. Dave heard splashes of paper, as if the man were flinging the files out of the drawers in a tearing hurry. The drawer slammed shut, another slid open. More papers were thrown. Dave opened the den door. The small man jerked around to stare at him. He was clean-shaven, with a big nose, eyes set close together. He was around fifty, and wore plaid trousers, a green cardigan sweater, a golf cap. "Who the hell are you?" he said. "What are you doing here?"

"That's no way to treat a man's files," Dave said.

The man's eyes narrowed. "Don't I know you from someplace? Insurance?"

"If you're Murray Berman, you do," Dave said. "I know one reason you're here—the family's at church. What's the other reason?"

"I'm looking for something of mine Drew had and I have to have back. It's no use to him now. And I don't want to have to hassle with lawyers to get it." He pushed his hands into the file drawer again.

Dave said, "Forget it, Murray. It's not in there." Dave bent to pick up file folders, spread sheets, manila envelopes from the floor. "Where you know me from is San Pedro, twenty years ago. An alleged warehouse robbery on the docks that turned out to be insurance fraud by a Chinatown importer. Remember? You sold the policy. I was the investigator—on loan to one of your Hartford companies from my company, Medallion."

"Right." Berman nodded, started to smile, changed his mind. "What do you mean, it's not here?"

Dave laid a stack of files, envelopes, papers in the short man's arms. "Put those back, will you?" Mutely, Berman did as he was told. Dave crouched to gather up more of the litter. "You were located in Long Beach in those days. Now you're in Thousand Oaks, right?" Dave laid his gleanings on the desk to straighten them. "Head of your own agency." He put the stack into Berman's hands. "Doing well, are you?"

"Close to half a million last year," Berman said. "Investigator. I see." He nodded, frowning to himself. "You been checking up on me. Why?"

"Matter of fact, I only began this morning." Dave was down on hands and knees now, reaching under the desk for papers that had slithered there. "Will you help me pick up this mess, please? You made it."

Berman stood where he was. "You've got the letter."

"I've got it." Shoulder hurting, Dave backed out from under the desk with the papers, climbed to his feet, handed the papers to Berman. "And I've read it."

"Oh, hell." Disgusted, Berman let the papers slip loosely from his hands into the drawer.

He slammed the drawer shut. He stood, facing nothing for a minute, then drew breath and faced Dave. "Look, it doesn't mean what it says. I was panicky. I shouldn't have mailed it. I wouldn't have except he was always out, never returned my calls." Berman held out small, plump, begging hands. "Give it back. Forget it. Why do you want to make trouble for me?"

"What kind of trouble?" Dave said. "You think if the police read it, they'd arrest you for Dodge's murder?"

Berman went pale. "I didn't threaten to kill him. Where's my letter? Let me show you."

"What you threatened," Dave said, "was to tell all his investors something you alone had found out—that Sears-Roebuck and Safeway supermarkets weren't coming into the shopping mall. The two biggest tenants Dodge had promised you all when he conned your money out of you had changed their minds. And without them, the mall would never earn you back a thin dime—none of you."

"I just wanted my part back," Berman said. "Drew was short of funds. Contractors and suppliers hadn't been paid in months. Drew had been sick in the hospital. The project was collapsing. I only wanted what was mine while the getting was good, before he could pull a chapter eleven on us, go bankrupt." Tears came to Berman's eyes. "Give me the letter." He fumbled to bring a checkbook from a hip pocket. "I'll pay you. Name your price."

"You're a real mensch, Murray," Dave said. "What did you care what happened to the other little guys like you, shopkeepers, automobile dealers, veterinarians, doctors, lawyers, dentists, teachers? Just so long as you got yours."

Berman didn't hear him. He dropped onto the swivel chair, switched on the desk lamp, opened the green leather checkbook folder, pulled the cap off a pen. He peered up at Dave, forehead wrinkled. "Ten thousand?"

"I don't want money," Dave said, "I want the truth."

"Wh-what about?" Berman stammered.

"Begin with what happened after Dodge got your letter."

"He phoned me to come see him." Berman held up the checkbook to Dave and looked pitiable. "Fifteen thousand?"

"Put it away, "Dave said. "You came to see him, right? And he gave you a lot of sweet talk, didn't he?"

"He looked awful—I hardly recognized him." Berman glumly pushed the pen into its slot in the folder, closed the folder, pushed it back into his hip pocket. "Thin and pale. And weak? Even his voice was weak. Yeah, we talked. Right in this room."

"He asked you to wait," Dave said. "He just knew he could turn Sears and Safeway around if you gave him time, right? Or did he say he'd hooked Montgomery Ward and Von's instead? What did he say, Murray?"

"How do you know so much?" Berman said.

"People have told me how he operated," Dave said.

"Yeah, well, I knew him, too, by then. And I wasn't buying. I wanted my money. I got real ugly with him, and he said he'd get it for me. He knew somebody he could hit up for it. He didn't say who."

"I think I know," Dave said. "Did he say when?"

"He tried leaving it vague," Berman said, "but I gave him a deadline."

"The night he was killed," Dave said.

Berman looked sick. "Who told you that?"

Dave inched him a smile. "I learned it just now, down on my hands and knees. Tell me how it went. You came at the appointed time. Here?"

Berman nodded. "By the back way. But not at the appointed time. Early. I didn't trust him."

"And you were right, yes? He was driving away, wasn't he? He wasn't going to be there when you arrived."

Berman gaped. "You were following me."

Dave shook his head. "This is the first time you've worn those shoes since that night, isn't it?"

"What?" Berman peered at the shoes, frowned up at Dave. "Yeah, I guess it is. What about it?"

"There are flowers stuck to them," Dave said. "Yellow once, brown now. From the trees on the street where Dodge was killed. You were sore, and you followed him—sixty miles down the freeway, and clear into East Hollywood. You parked behind him on the street, and braced him for your money."

"He didn't have it, but he had a gun. And I wasn't getting shot. Not for all the money in the world."

"So you ran back to your car and drove off? You didn't see a skinny teenager confront Dodge in the parking space under the apartments across the street?"

"My back was turned. I heard the gun go off, and I saw this kid running away. Didn't see Drew anyplace. Figured he'd scared the kid like he scared me. Why did he go there?"

"He had a friend in those apartments," Dave said. "The kid—you didn't know him? Never saw him before?"

"What? You mean here, in the valley? His kind don't show up out here. No, I never saw him before."

"What color was his car, did you notice?"

"Dark—blue, brown?" Berman shrugged. "It was an old wreck from the sixties—Chevette or something."

"License number?" Dave said.

"It was too dark," Berman said. "Anyway, who cared?"

Tires crunched the gravel of the drive out front. Berman jumped up. "That's the family home from the funeral." Car doors slammed. Women's voices broke the morning stillness. Shrill. Arguing. "I'm out of here," Berman said, yanked the den door open, vanished down the hallway. Dave moved after him, taking his time.

"You are too going," Kathy Dodge cried.

"I'm not, and that's that," said Gerda Nilson. "I'm not deserting my child when she's sick and dying."

"Mother, you can't save me." The house door burst open. The voices were clearer now. "We've been all over this. Look at the clock. You'll miss the plane."

"We'll all stay here together," Gerda Nilson said.

"No. I'm not putting the children through that. The cruelty's already started at school. Take them to Minneapolis now. You promised. I'll clear things up here, sell the house, and come along back there as soon as I can."

Gerda Nilson's voice was harsh with tears. "I could kill that man for what he did to you." Dave stepped down into the lanai and pulled the house door shut behind him.

17

THE SHADOW OF the church had turned and shortened. It fell on the cars in the parking lot now, Dave's brown Jaguar, and the off-white LAPD car. The detective with the moustache stood beside this one, smoking a cigarette, and talking to Tom Owens. Owens had shed the trenchcoat but still wore the Irish hat. Dave parked the BMW, took the keys from the ignition, climbed out of the car, slammed the door, and walked over to the men.

"They said you were slippery." The detective pulled out a handkerchief and wiped his nose. "But you shouldn't have done it to me." He pushed the handkerchief away. "You shouldn't have involved Mr. Owens, here. You know that."

"And I apologize," Dave said. "But let's count our blessings—I wasn't shot and I wasn't stabbed." He brought out the letters—both typewritten on crisp stationery—and peered at them. The one with Berman's letterhead he passed to the detective. "Call Lieutenant Leppard about this man. He'll want to question him."

The detective sneezed. "Damn. I think I'm getting a cold." He got the handkerchief out again, sneezed again, blew his nose, put the handkerchief away. He dropped his cigarette, stepped on it, read the letter and blinked at Dave, tilting his head. "Where did you get this?"

"You don't want me to answer that," Dave said. "Berman came after it himself. I got it just in time."

"I'm sketchy on the case," the detective said. "What does it mean?"

Dave told him what it meant, and added, "He may be lying about the boy. He may have hired the boy to scare Dodge. And the gun made it turn out wrong."

"I'll go myself," the detective said. He shook Dave's hand. "Morales," he said. He walked around to the driver side of the car, opened the door, paused. "Where do I catch up with you?"

"The Oaktree Inn. I'll light there sometime."

Morales nodded. "I'll spot your car. There aren't a lot like it. Be careful, now, all right?"

"Arrest Berman, why don't you?" Dave said. "The scare might do him good. Witnesses to murder are supposed to come forward. Aren't they?"

"I can't arrest him," Morales said. "Wrong jurisdiction. I'll turn him over to the local authority, whoever that is."

"County sheriff," Dave said. "The station faces the town square. On the west side."

"Thanks." Morales got into his car. The motor thrashed raggedly to life. He backed out of the parking slot, clanked the gears, rolled onto the empty highway.

"I thought you'd never come back," Tom Owens said.

"I'm sorry to have worried you," Dave said. "I hope Morales didn't get too unpleasant."

"Only with himself." Owens grinned. "Nobody likes to be made a fool of. He cussed himself out. Spanish is not invariably the loving tongue." He passed the hat back to Dave, ran fingers through his hair. "Where did you go?"

Dave told him. "Dodge gave his wife AIDS."

"Dear God," Owens said. "He can't have meant to. Can he?" The yellow eyes pleaded for an assurance no one could give. "It's easy to have it and not know. That's what's so horrible about it."

"One of the things that's so horrible about it." Dave laid the BMW keys in Owens's hand. "Thanks for your help. It was even more important than I thought."

"You're not coming back with me to the beach?"

"I'd like that," Dave said. "Thanks. But there's another of Dodge's victims I have to talk to."

"You really going to put up at a motel?" Owens gazed around him at the valley, the green hills hemming it in, the emptiness. "With television for company?"

"Not if I can help it," Dave said. "Tell Larry to mat those watercolors of his he's got in the workroom. I want to buy them."

Owens's face lit up. "He'll be thrilled." He moved off to the BMW and got inside. "That's a nice gesture."

"It's no gesture." Dave walked to him, fitting on the hat. "When I got home, I'd regret I hadn't brought them along. Didn't you ever see anything, and know you couldn't be happy without it?"

"Yes—Larry." Owens laughed, closed the car door, then rolled the window down, stuck out a hand. "Almost forgot your keys. We'll see you then, on your way home?"

"I like to think so." Dave took the keys, backed away from the BMW. Smiling, Owens started it up, reversed it, guided it out of the silent parking lot onto the empty highway. It headed south after Morales. Dave watched it diminish, then went to a telephone sheltered by an open-sided glass-and-steel box next to the rear door of the church. He put in a collect call to Amanda at her busy shop on Rodeo Drive, and after that to Cecil at the apartment in Mar Vista. To tell them where he was, so they wouldn't worry if they found the place on Horseshoe Canyon Trail empty. They asked for explanations. He didn't explain. "But I think it's nearly over. You develop a sense about these things, after a while. I'm getting close."

"Be careful," Amanda said. "Are the police with you?"

"Detective Morales," Dave said. "Don't worry."

"How do I get there?" Cecil said. "Wait for me. You shouldn't be alone."

"I'm glad you realize that," Dave said, and hung up.

Tall, blond, gangly, a figure in white tennis shorts, white short-sleeved shirt, lobbed a fuzzy yellow ball across a green net. Rubber soles squeaked on the composition surface of the court. The player on the far side was a boy of maybe thirteen, blond also, cream- skinned, blue-eyed, but he hadn't got his growth yet, nor lost his baby fat. The hair of the tall one was long and straight and held by a headband. When little brother ignored the ball, let it bounce past him to the tall hedge that backed the yard, and pointed his racket at Dave, she turned. It was a she. Maybe seventeen. She squinted in the sun glare.

"Can I help you?"

"Senator Bud Hollywell," Dave said. "I telephoned his office in Sacramento. They said he was at home."

"He's talking to a businessmen's luncheon," she said, "in Agoura Hills." She read a tiny gold watch on a skinny wrist. "He won't be home for hours."

Dave took out his wallet, thumbed a card from it, handed it to her. "Give him this, will you please? Tell him to expect me back. When? Around dinnertime?"

"I guess so," she said, shook back her hair, gave him a smile of straight, white teeth. She wore no makeup, her chest was flat, her hips narrow. In jeans, she could pass herself off as a boy with no trouble. "I'll give it to him," she said. "What's it about?"

"The death of Drew Dodge," Dave said.

Her face clouded. She glanced over her shoulder. Her brother was poking around the roots of the hedge, looking for the ball. She said softly to Dave, "Did you know he was gay? He had AIDS?"

"If I hadn't already known it," Dave said, "I'd have guessed it at the funeral. Nobody came."

"My father had this luncheon meeting. It's a long drive. There wasn't time."

"Do you know if he'd seen Mr. Dodge lately?" Dave said. "After Dodge got out of the hospital—just before he was killed? Had he come here to see your father? On business?"

"It would have had to be on business," she said. "They weren't friends or anything." She stressed this. She didn't want a stranger getting wrong ideas about her father. "I don't think he came here. I didn't see him."

"Do you go down to Los Angeles a lot?" Dave said.

"What for?" She made a face. "The smog?"

"I just had an idea I'd seen you in Los Angeles lately."

"Not me." She gave her head a firm shake. Her long hair swung. "We moved here years ago to get away from all that. This is lovely. I'll never go back."

"Ma-til-da!" Her brother had found the tennis ball, and stood bouncing it with his racket. "Are we playing tennis or what? I can always go back to my computer, you know."

"Just a minute," she called.

"You like sports," Dave said. "Do you take any defense training, karate, that kind of thing?"

"I'm too tall for my age group," she said. "You have to be the right size to match up with the other kids. I'm never the right size. For anything."

"What about knife fighting?" Dave looked away, at treetops, at the sky. "Anyone around here teach that?"

"Knife fighting?" She gave an audible shudder. "No. I never heard of anything like that. Not in this valley."

"It's cattle country," Dave said. "Knives are standard equipment in cattle country."

"No. I never did any knife fighting. Who are you, anyway? What kind of question is that?"

"If you don't know"—Dave smiled at her—"then I'm sorry for asking." He turned to leave, turned back. "But it's important I see your father. He wrote a letter to Drew Dodge. He'll want to explain it."

"My father is a fine man," she flared. "A wonderful man. Don't you go making any trouble for him."

"I'll be back around five." Dave walked away.

The slow *pock, pock* of the tennis ball took up again behind him.

The name of the paper was lettered in Gothic inside a plate of glass that fronted the offices. THE WEATHERVANE. The lettering formed an arc over a drawing in black and gold of a weathervane. Nothing like spelling things out for the folks. The office was a storefront that faced the town square. Across the square, beyond the big dark old trees and the seesaws, swings, jungle gyms, beyond the boys teetering on skateboards around the lacy steel band pavilion, rose the hardware store, Drew Dodge's lifeless offices above it. To Dave's left, catty corner, the sheriff 's substation was housed in brown brick.

A counter crossed the front room of the newspaper offices. Beyond desks that held computer terminals or typewriters and slag heaps of paper was a Masonite partition. When Dave stood at the counter, where advertising rate sheets covered in yellowing plastic were fastened down with aged and curling transparent tape, he saw a pressroom through an opening in the partition. Offset presses whirred. A young man with a boil on the nape of his neck rattled the keyboard of a typesetting computer.

A man got up from a desk and came to the counter. He was stocky, wore plain steel-rim spectacles and a bushy red beard. He was bald on top, but the fringe of hair he still had grew long down over the collar of his checkered wool shirt. Dave took him for about forty. The 1960s had formed him. That was what his appearance said. He smiled with small, badly aligned teeth. It was the smile of a man naturally cheerful, naturally optimistic. That was, of course, too easy a judgment. Anybody trying to make a living off operating a small-town weekly newspaper simply had to be like that. "What can I do for you?" he said.

"Pete McCaffrey?" Dave held out the folder with his private investigator's license in it. "I'm making some inquiries into the death of Drew Dodge. They tell me you were good friends."

McCaffrey dropped the smile. Not out of decorum. "Look," he said, "I didn't know he was gay. Never. He never dropped a hint."

"I didn't see you at the funeral," Dave said.

"It's—it's publication day. Busiest day of my week. We go to press tonight. I have easy days. But not this one. I was here at five this morning. I'll be here till five tomorrow morning. No way could I get to the church."

"I don't think you'd have gone if it was an easy day," Dave said. "I think you're scared of what people would think."

McCaffrey grimaced. "That's one of the joys of running a small-town paper. If you look cross-eyed at somebody, they pull their advertising."

"And if they got even the faintest idea that you were gay because of your association with Drew Dodge—?"

McCaffrey drew a stubby finger across his thick throat. "Yeah. Right. It makes a man ashamed of himself. Time was when I wouldn't have given a damn."

"When you wrote for the LA *Free Press!*" Dave grinned.

McCaffrey snorted. "It was *Open City,* but you've got the idea. Yeah, if I was dying, I'd have crawled out of bed to go to that funeral. Shit." He wagged his head.

"Let me guess—you've got a family to support," Dave said. "Responsibilities. You have to think of consequences now. The years make us cautious."

"Yeah, well, it's nice of you to put it that way," McCaffrey said, "but I'm not proud of myself."

A sixtyish woman, straw-colored hair pulled up on her head, had been rattling away at one of the scarred IBM Selectrics on a desk, copying from a dog-eared pocket notebook. Now she took off her half-moon glasses, rose, and came to McCaffrey with a question. When she'd gone back to her desk, the telephone on the counter rang, and

McCaffrey talked into it for a while. Dave turned and watched small children in red and green padded jackets and jeans swing in the park. He also saw Morales lead an arm-waving Murray Berman into the sheriff 's office. McCaffrey hung up, read his watch.

"What's on your mind?" he said. "I have to get to work."

"Dodge left an envelope with you, didn't he," Dave said, "only days before he was killed? What did it say on it—'To be opened in case of my death?'"

McCaffrey took a step backward. "Jesus," he said. "Who the hell are you, anyway? How did you know that?"

"I didn't. I'm guessing. But I'm guessing right, no? Is that what was written on it?"

"Nothing was written on it," McCaffrey said. "He just gave it to me and said, 'Keep this, Pete, and if anything should happen to me, open it and publish it.'"

"Something happened to him," Dave said. "Did you publish it?"

"I forgot all about it," McCaffrey said. "When he brought it in out of the rain, it was one of those days like today. My mind was on a thousand details here, and we had a computer breakdown, and the repairman was late." He went to his desk, pulled open a rattly drawer. "I dropped it in here and didn't think any more about it." He rummaged an envelope out from others in the drawer, banged the drawer shut, brought the envelope back to the counter, scowling at it. DREW DODGE ASSOCIATES was printed in the upper left corner. The red-bearded man turned the envelope over and over in his fingers. He peered through the little lenses at Dave. "Do you think I ought to open it? Maybe I ought to phone my lawyer. Maybe I should give it to the sheriff."

"What for? It was you he handed it to. Open it. Maybe there's a scoop in it."

McCaffrey eyed Dave uneasily. "You know what's in it?"

"Not for sure. But I'd bet on a Xerox of a letter to Dodge from Senator Bud Hollywell."

"Oh, Christ." McCaffrey lost some of his ruddiness.

"Asking Dodge to return the money Hollywell invested in the shopping mall project." Dave watched the editor closely. "I expect you can tell me why."

"I—I don't know what you mean," McCaffrey said.

"If you don't," Dave said, "then you're a very unusual newspaperman." He glanced around the shop. "They always know more than they print. Rumor. Gossip. Leaks they can't get witnesses to commit to." He tilted his head. "Hollywell is headed for trouble. Isn't that right?"

"I've—heard something like that," McCaffrey said.

"He was a shoo-in at the last election," Dave said. "Like ninety percent of the incumbents, if they want the job again it's theirs, isn't it? The two who ran against him advertised and campaigned like crazy and got nowhere. He had a bulging war chest and hardly had to crack it."

McCaffrey gave in. He nodded. "Bulging with seven hundred fifty thousand dollars. It's on record."

"What's not on record," Dave said, "is that he turned half a million of it over to Drew Dodge for the shopping mall project. Invested it. Expecting a high return. That's what Dodge promised you all, wasn't it? Meantime, the campaign money was just sitting there. Nobody'd know the difference. It wouldn't be counted again until the next election."

"Except the election commission decided to audit it," McCaffrey said. "That what you're getting at?"

"Is that the rumor?" Dave said.

McCaffrey nodded grimly. "That's the rumor."

"Dodge wasn't in a position to pay it back," Dave said. "And Dodge also knew there was two hundred fifty thousand more where Hollywell had gotten the first half million. He was being pressed hard to pay contractors and suppliers. And at least one other investor was threatening to ruin him if Dodge didn't give him back his hundred thousand."

McCaffrey squinted. "You saying Drew went to Hollywell asking for more?"

"Didn't he?" Dave said. "You knew him. You were his friend, whether you like the sound of that or not. I'm told he had a gift when it came to getting money out of people. Never worried about it. Knew just how to go after it, just where and when to ask. And never came up empty."

McCaffrey gave a sad, one-cornered smile. "Yeah, I guess that kind of sums him up, all right." He remembered and frowned at the envelope again. "You mean he threatened that I'd print the facts about Bud's misusing those funds for his own profit?"

"Unless Hollywell forked over the balance," Dave said. "He had to go to Hollywell, the way I hear it. The rest of you had given him your last dime already."

"I sure as hell had," McCaffrey said. He snorted, shook his head, used a thumb to pry up the flap of the envelope, making a ragged tear. He drew out two pages and read them. He looked at Dave with grim admiration. "You win your bet. But it was some sicko who killed Drew. Down in LA. It wasn't Bud Hollywell."

"What do you know about his daughter?"

"Matilda?" McCaffrey frowned. "What about her?"

"Tall skinny kid with long hair. A witness saw someone like that where Dodge was killed just before his death."

McCaffrey winced. "Jesus, you've got some kind of mind."

"Is she wild? Ever been in trouble?"

McCaffrey unhappily rubbed a hand over his bald dome. "Okay. School vandalism once, years ago. Lately—there were some break-ins around here. Shops. Liquor missing, little stuff like that. But she's an important man's daughter. The sheriff didn't want to make waves. He rang Sacramento for Mom to come and get her. You know how it is."

"Drugs?" Dave asked. "Thefts of items she could sell to support a habit?"

"She's not even seventeen yet," McCaffrey protested.

"They start at eleven these days," Dave said.

"No. The sheriff never said anything about drugs," McCaffrey said. "Listen, are you seriously trying to tell me a child like Matilda Hollywell would go out and stab somebody to death on a dark street?"

"Does she own her own car?"

"Every kid in Rancho Vientos owns a car by the time they're old enough to get a driver's license."

"And she does run around without parental supervision— right? Father and mother go up to Sacramento for days at a time together, leaving the kids alone?"

"With the cleaning woman," McCaffrey said. "Sheriff tells me they want her to go up with them, but she refuses. Smashes up her room and so on. But this is an insane conversation, Brandstetter. Bud Hollywell? Tell his own daughter to go kill an enemy for him? Come on!"

Dave said, "Maybe she acted on her own. Worships her father. Overheard Dodge threatening him. Wasn't going to let anyone bring down her hero."

"I'm glad I don't think like you," McCaffrey said.

"So you're not going to print the letters," Dave said.

"Not without confirmation," McCaffrey said.

"I'm going to brace him this afternoon. Come along."

"No way. I want no part of it till it's proved."

18

DAVE LEFT THE Jaguar where it was, crossed the square, and found the narrow passageway of shops Judith Ober had led him down what seemed a long time ago. Today the shops had customers, buying belts and handbags, serapes and junk jewelry, fancy coffees and teas. Tourists. Sunglasses, sundresses. Men in checked trousers like Murray Berman's. Cameras on straps around their necks. Dave remembered a set of three pay phones someplace along here. He found them. Luckily, no one was phoning home to check on the kids. Maybe they all knew it was no use anymore. Like the Hollywells. He dug out his plastic call card to get Mel Fleischer in LA.

Tall, balding, patrician, Fleischer was a senior vice president of a big California bank that had recently grown much bigger, swallowing up first one, then a second, then a third chain of banks in five states. Mel was a genius at what he did, making money earn money, his own as well as other people's. He lived well, but he also gave lavishly to the museum, the Philharmonic, and lesser cultural projects that kept musicians, actors, artists off welfare. He collected the work of California painters, mainly Millard Sheets, and paid the rent and grocery bills for promising newcomers, if their stuff wasn't too farfetched. He and Dave had been lovers when the world was new and strange. At present, Mel lived with a Japanese graduate student called Makoto. It kept him young.

"What I need, I need in a hurry," Dave said, "and it may not be easy to get."

Fleischer laughed. "What else is new? Does he bank with us or a competitor?"

"There's only one bank in Rancho Vientos, and it's yours," Dave said. "But that doesn't mean he uses the same bank in Sacramento. He's a state senator, Charles Emmett Hollywell, affectionately known as Bud." Dave spelled out the story. "I need confirmation of the withdrawal."

"Fascinating," Fleischer said. "Do the voters ever elect men of honor anymore?"

"I haven't heard of one lately," Dave said.

"I'll get back to you," Fleischer said. "Where?"

"I'm on the move," Dave said. "Better leave word at Tom Owens's."

"Not with friend Cecil?" Fleischer sounded surprised. And avid. "Don't tell me you've broken up."

"All right," Dave said, "I won't tell you. He's spending time with a young lady these days. I don't know when it will end. I'm beginning to wonder if it ever will."

"Too bad," Fleischer said. "He's a dear boy. Well—I never did understand sex. And I fear I never shall."

"Keep working on it," Dave said. "Listen, thanks for your help. We'll have dinner at Max's when this is over."

"I'll look forward to it," Fleischer said.

Dave walked to the end of the passageway and into the little café with its blonde tables, bentwood chairs, hanging plants. Sun shone cheerfully through the skylight today. When Dave and Judith Ober had the place to themselves, rain had pattered up there. Today, the ranch-hand waiter with the sunburned nose had to stumble around among a lot of butchers. Dave had to wait for a table. He leaned on the small bar and drank Glenlivet. His shoulder ached, and he was thankful for the breather. This was getting to be quite a day.

Katherine Dodge didn't look sick. She looked better than on the first morning he'd seen her. She'd changed her black funeral dress for jeans, a gingham shirt, and had piled her hair on top of her head, carelessly, not expecting anyone. She squinted in the sunlight at the open front door, plainly not sure just who he was, but thinking she ought to remember. He freshened her memory.

"Oh, yes." Her smile was faint. "I was in shock. I don't know that I'm out of shock yet. What do you want?"

"The police in LA know now that it wasn't the serial killer who murdered your husband. Are you aware of that?"

"From the news." She pulled wet latex gloves off her thin hands. "It was a tall blond boy with long hair." Her eyes cleared. "Ah. He attacked you, too, didn't he?"

"He seems to think I know something that can hurt him. He's wrong. I'm asking around Rancho Vientos today to try and find out what it could be, who he is."

"I don't know," she said, "but I think I may have seen him once. Someone who answers that description, anyway."

Dave blinked. "You didn't tell the police?"

"They haven't been back. I gather there's a dispute with the sheriff about who has jurisdiction in the case. I only remembered the boy now. You reminded me. Come in?"

"You're busy," Dave said. "I don't want to keep you. Where did you see this boy? When?"

"Sunset time. The day Drew appeared on that LA talk show. He was excited about it and, of course, I missed it, wouldn't you know? The children had gone on a field trip from school. The bus broke down. They were hours late getting back. I was stuck waiting at the school. With all the other mothers. I rushed to apologize to Drew. I felt awful about it. He wasn't in his den. I went out to the lanai. And saw him out by the pool, talking to this

159

ragged, long-haired teenager. I stepped outside, called to Drew, and the boy started toward me. Drew grabbed his arm, spoke sharply to him, and the boy went away out the back gate.

"I'm told you don't have his sort in Rancho Vientos."

"No, that's true, we don't," she said. "But we did that time, didn't we?"

"Maybe not. Do you know Bud Hollywell's daughter?"

"Slightly. Matilda." She brushed a fallen strand of hair off her face. And frowned. "Ah. I see. Tall, blonde, long-haired. Do I think it was Matilda? Dressed like that?"

"Kids put on funny clothes these days," Dave said. "They pay high prices for wrinkles, rips, and wrong sizes."

"I know." But she shook her head. "I asked Drew who it was. A boy wanting yard work, he said, to clean the pool, trim the trees."

"And you believed that?"

Her laugh was brief and bitter. "I believed whatever Drew Dodge told me. Then. I learned better, didn't I, but not till it was too late. He lied all the time, damn him." Tears came into her eyes. Her mouth trembled. She gave her head an impatient shake, angry at the tears, the self-reproach. "His whole life was a lie."

"Tell me about his life. Where did he come from? Who were his parents? Where did he go to school?"

"He wouldn't talk about the past. He said none of it mattered. All that mattered was now, the two of us. I wasn't raised to pry. I loved him. We were happy. I was a fool."

"The past came to get him," Dave said. "He told Tom Owens that, the architect. The night before he was killed. Somebody surfaced, demanding money to keep quiet about that past that didn't matter. Owens didn't know how to help, so he gave him my business card."

"And that's how he came to be at your house. Where you found him that morning. Dead."

"That's how." The sun was high, it was a whiter sun, but it had a little warmth to it now. Dave took off the tweed hat and stuffed it into a side pocket of his jacket. He said, "Your mother told me he wouldn't have his picture taken. Yet he agreed to be on television. Didn't it occur to him that amounted to the same thing? Cameras?"

Her mouth opened slightly. "My God, you're right. No, he didn't think of it. Neither did I. Or mother. We'd have said something. Teased him. And he wouldn't have done it. Never. It was a phobia with him." She eyed Dave anxiously. "Is it important? It is, isn't it?"

"Unless that was Matilda Hollywell you saw."

"I don't understand," she said.

"Neither do I," Dave said. "Not yet."

Clouds came from the west, from beyond the ridges that cut the valley off from the ocean. The temperature dropped and the wind picked up. He drove into the new gas station at the place where the road left the highway and wound up into the expensive houses on the eastward hills. He left the Jaguar to be fueled at a row of shiny square blue and yellow pumps, and went to find a phone. Two of them, bracketed by steel-framed glass, were fastened to the outside wall of the station office. He used his card to get the number he wanted. The phone rang in his ear. Out on the highways cars swished past. Up on the green hills, reading the weather, cattle began to move slowly toward the shelter of old oaks. Inside the station, a boom box thundered rock music. Larry Johns answered the phone.

Dave said, "Are you matting those watercolors for me? The ones tacked up in your workroom? I want to buy them."

"What? Really?" Johns sounded much like the adolescent boy he'd been twelve years ago when Dave first met him. "Hey, that's very nice of you, Mr. Brandstetter. Sure, I'll get started on them right away."

"I take it Tom isn't there," Dave said. "I thought he was with you."

Dave told him when they'd parted at the church.

"That's funny," Johns said. "There's nothing on his calendar today. He should have been here hours ago. He always phones if he changes his plans. He knows I worry."

"Then he'll be there soon, I expect," Dave said. "Any messages for me?"

"Oh, yes. Sorry. You shook me up about the pictures. You don't have to buy them. Let me give them to you. I owe you a lot more than that. You saved my ass."

"I like the pictures," Dave said, "and I want them, but I can't take them if you won't let me pay you for them. Don't spoil it for me."

Johns laughed. "Okay. I won't spoil it for you."

"Was it Mel Fleischer who called?"

"About forty-five minutes ago. I didn't understand exactly what it all meant, but I wrote it down. Just a second." The phone clanked against something. Papers lisped. Johns picked up the phone again. "He said Bud Hollywell does have accounts in the Western States branch in Sacramento. Two. A personal account, and a campaign fund account. And on November twelfth, like you said, he did transfer money from the campaign fund to his personal account. And the next day he withdrew that money."

"In cash," Dave said.

"You got it," Johns said. "Half a million bucks." He sounded a little awed. "Who is this guy?"

"One of our esteemed public servants," Dave said.

"Sounds more like a drug dealer," Johns said.

"Drug dealers aren't as dangerous," Dave said. "Thank you. Tell Tom I hope to see you in a couple of hours."

"Yeah. Good. I hope he gets here soon. It's starting to rain."

It was starting to rain on Dave, too. He paid for the gas, got back into the Jaguar, and drove off.

A big maroon Cadillac sat on the curved drive at the Hollywell house. The house had no style. Sterile arches. Showy double entrance doors. Not a window to be seen. Shrubs neatly trimmed to boxy shapes. On the flagstone doorstep stood an attaché case and what Dave judged to be a case for a lap computer. He got out of the Jaguar, dragging the trenchcoat after him. He put this on, hurting his shoulder. One of the double doors opened, and a lean man came out, white raincoat over a tweed jacket and wool slacks, shirt and tie. A small leather suitcase was in his hand. When he saw Dave, he stopped dead.

"You're early," he said.

"And you planned not to be here when I arrived." Dave walked to him and held out a hand. "Brandstetter."

"Yeah, well, I have an emergency call from my office at the capital," Bud Hollywell said. "We'll have to meet at a later date."

"I'll fly up with you," Dave said. "I have nothing important to do."

Hollywell brushed past him, unlocked the trunk of the Cadillac, threw in the suitcase. "I'm driving." He went back for the two smaller cases, set them in the trunk, shut down the lid of the trunk, withdrew the keys. "Sorry."

"We should discuss this letter." Dave took it from inside his jacket, rattled it at Hollywell. "It could make any more trips to Sacramento superfluous for you."

Hollywell narrowed his eyes. He half reached out to snatch the letter, but thought better of it. "Matilda said something about a letter I'd supposedly written Drew Dodge. Is that it? Where did you get it?"

"That doesn't matter now. What matters is what the letter says. It says you'd invested half a million dollars in the shopping mall project. Now you had to have it back. The money came from your campaign fund. And that fund was about to be audited."

"I never wrote such a letter," Hollywell said. "How could I? It's a lie, a frame-up. I know you're the best in your profession. I've seen you on TV, read about you in magazines. But you don't know politics. It's a very specialized field, and sometimes a very dirty one. I had opponents in this last race who'd do anything to stop me."

"I believe it," Dave said, "but what I'm interested in is what you'd do to stop Drew Dodge. Someone stopped him. You'll agree with that."

"Some mugger, a senseless street killing." Hollywell winched up at the rain, moved off. "And this is a senseless conversation." Fitting the key into the lock, he glanced scornfully at Dave. "Stop Drew Dodge from what?"

"From telling the world where that half million came from you'd invested in his project for your own profit."

"He wouldn't have dared. That letter is a forgery."

Dave shook his head. "I've had your bank records in Sacramento checked out, Senator. The date of the withdrawal was in November, only a week after you got re-elected. You transferred the money from the campaign fund to your personal account, then withdrew it next day. In cash."

"There's no way to trace where it went." Hollywell's face was white, and his hand shook so the car keys rattled in it. "You can't prove I gave that money to Dodge."

"I expect his records will show it," Dave said. "You can bet those records will be thoroughly checked out by the police or the sheriff in the next few days. A half million dollars in cash is hard to conceal."

Hollywell pulled open the car door. "This is pure speculation on your part. I haven't time for this." He got into the car, slammed the door, glared out at Dave as the window came down. "You show that letter, and everyone will know it for what it is. A fake, meant to discredit me. It won't work. The voters trust me."

Dave said, "Pete McCaffrey has a copy of the letter. Dodge gave it to him in a sealed envelope. With instructions to print it if anything happened to him."

"Well, something happened to him, all right," Hollywell said, "and McCaffrey didn't print it, did he? You want to know why? Because he knows me better than you do. He knows that letter can't be legitimate."

"He knows you? Or he's afraid of you? Or is it the same thing?" Dave asked. "He's only waiting for more proof, Senator. Those bank statements will help."

"Just what is it you want?" Hollywell said.

"I want to know who killed Drew Dodge," Dave said, "and who slashed me with a knife a couple of nights later because I'd been out here to Rancho Vientos nosing around, getting too close to the answer."

"Well, I didn't kill him," Hollywell said. He pushed the key into the ignition. Dave reached into the car, grabbed his hand, wrenched the keys away from him. "What the hell do you think you're doing?"

"We haven't finished our conversation," Dave said. "There's more. After Dodge left the letter with McCaffrey, he came to you. In the rain. Like today. And he told you he would use that letter against you unless you coughed up the two hundred fifty thousand still sitting in the campaign fund. He'd been a long time in the hospital. Contractors and suppliers were demanding their money. Worse than that, an investor called Murray Berman had found out Sears-Roebuck and Safeway stores weren't coming into the mall, and was going to tell all the rest of you, if Dodge didn't give him back his money. Dodge told Berman he knew someone he could hit up for the money. It was you, wasn't it?"

"He tried," Hollywell said. "I laughed at him."

"And then you went and had a heart-to-heart talk with your daughter, right?"

Hollywell jerked with surprise. "What? Matilda? What the hell has she got to do with this?"

"You tell me. You couldn't give Dodge what he asked for. You knew this audit was coming. You were facing problems enough rigging receipts to convince the auditors that the half million went for campaign debts. But you also couldn't let Dodge go public with the truth. He had to be stopped. A tall, skinny adolescent with long blond hair and a knife stopped him."

Hollywell made an animal sound, burst out of the car, lunged at Dave, fists flailing. Dave stepped aside, put out a foot, and tripped him. He went sprawling on the rain-wet tarmac of the drive. Dave said, "Beating up a man twenty years your senior isn't going to help your image, Senator."

Hollywell didn't answer. He pushed up off the paving slowly, sullen. He wiped his hands on a handkerchief, put it away, brushed at the sleeves of his white raincoat. He said between clenched teeth, "I apologize. But it's one thing to say outrageous things about me. I'm used to it. It comes with the job. It's another thing to attack a man's family."

"I only surmised," Dave said. "You attacked."

"Matilda wasn't even in the State of California when Drew Dodge was killed," Hollywell said. "Or when you were wounded. She'd gotten into serious trouble, here. Running with a pack of spoiled, rich brats we'd warned her against. Robberies. Can you imagine that? For the thrill of it, the mischief of it. What the hell is this generation coming to?"

"Where was she, exactly?" Dave said.

"At my mother's, in Seattle," Hollywell said. "We sent her up there to calm down and come to her senses. She always was a handful. But I think Mother straightened her out. I hope so. You phone Mrs. Virginia Hollywell in Seattle. It's a listed number. She'll confirm that Matilda was with her. And now, I'd like my keys back."

Dave handed them to him. "What are you going to do when McCaffrey publishes that letter?"

"Worried about me, now, are you?" Hollywell got into his car, slammed the door, started the engine. "I'm touched. But save your pity. McCaffrey hasn't got the guts. As for you—tomorrow you'll have forgotten all about me. I don't figure in your case, right?" The window rolled up and began to collect raindrops. Hollywell drove off.

19

THE WOMAN IN tight jeans, cowboy boots, a red and yellow satin cowboy shirt was painted up to look young. "We don't rent units," she said in a country western accent, "we rent suites." She slid a registration card to him. Her nails were long. The blood-red color would have been okay at roundup time, but the nails would have broken branding the first calf. Her hair was crow black. Her teeth were capped. The strip of neckerchief around her stringy throat was fastened by a bolo crusted with tiny glass emeralds, rubies, diamonds. Her cufflinks matched this. She blinked sooty false lashes. "No luggage, Mr—uh—Branflakes?" She grinned, a good old boy.

He grinned back. "Brandstetter," he said.

"Oh, hey," she said, "we've been waiting for you." She turned to a set of pigeonholes and pulled squares of paper from one. "It got mysterious, you know. I mean, you didn't have no reservation, and we says, 'Who is this, getting all these phone messages?'"

Dave frowned, accepted the memo slips, read Tom Owens's name on them, nodded, tucked them away. He was tired and disgusted and he already had the news he would get if he returned the architect's calls. "My luggage is in the car. I'll handle it, thanks." He bent under the crooked branch of a leafless, varnished mesquite bush on the counter, and put his name, address, license number on the card. He pushed the card at the woman, showed her his American Express card and driver's license. She passed him an Oaktree Inn key, studying him, sharp lines between her drawn-on brows. "I seen you on TV. That's where. Don't tell me I'm wrong. I never forget a face."

"I won't tell you you're wrong." He turned away.

"One of them talk shows, I bet," she called.

"You win." Dave pushed out into the damp day that was darkening fast, and went to find his room. Two rooms. One to sit and be lonely in, the other to lie down and be lonely in. Both smelled of new paint and carpet. When he switched on lamps, the windowpanes gleamed with a high shine. He closed the curtains. The wallpaper was unexciting. The pictures were watercolors of cattle, horses, windmills, barns. Television sets sat in both rooms. New glossy travel magazines lay on a coffee table. In a corner, a low cabinet held small bottles in a drawer. He crouched and through his reading glasses saw that there was no Glenlivet. There was Chivas. That would do. He unwrapped a glass in the bathroom, cracked the metal twist-off cap on the tiny bottle, poured what it held into the glass, added a couple of drops of water from the very new faucet of the very new basin that still had flecks of grout in it left behind by tilers.

He went back to the sitting room and fooled for two minutes with the dial of the stereo receiver built into the television cabinet. But the only available radio stations broadcast either country western or twangy gospel music. Cassettes lay in the glove compartment of the Jaguar, but he had nothing to play them on in here. He must buy a Walkman and keep it for times like this. He switched the noise off, dropped into a chair, lit a cigarette and listened to the rain falling outside. Good music. Some of the best.

The chair was not spacious. The tweed hat bulged in the side pocket of his jacket. He yanked it out, and a piece of grubby paper came with it, fluttered to the rug. Frowning, he tossed the hat onto the coffee table, set down his drink, picked up the paper. He had to dig out the reading glasses again. He smoothed the paper on his knee. It was rumpled. The writing was childish, rain-stained.

I cant wait no longer. You promised Friday nite and I waited in the dam rain for hours and you never come. You owe me and you no it is a rightfull dett and only a devil would treat"—here rain had washed the words out—*"I mean it. I will tell if you make me. A hunnerd thousand aint nowheres near enuf for what I been threw but I will settle for it and it aint much to you. Not to sackerfice your hole future for is it? It don't mean—*

Dave turned the page over. Nothing. The rest of the message was on another crumpled sheet someplace in those tossed files in Drew Dodge's dusty, deserted den. Maybe two sheets, or three—words flowed from the writer, pumped by anger, resentment, self-pity. He'd have to make do with one page. And the images in his mind of that angular figure, tense with fury, striking at him in the darkness and the rain, and the same ragged figure, this time with a gun, running away from Samuels between those sunset-bloodied apartment buildings, long hair flying.

He drank slowly, smoked the cigarette down. There was more—Katherine Dodge's memory of the tall, skinny kid talking to her husband out by his swimming pool late on the afternoon of the day Dodge had shown his handsome, wasted face to the world on television. The kid had started toward the woman, the man had stopped him, roughly, sent him away. What had the kid wanted to say to the woman? *This bastard,* Tom Owens had said, *wanted big bucks.* For what?

He read the note again, grunted, tossed it onto the table, put away his glasses. He went to the cabinet, bent for another bottle, emptied it into the empty glass, dropped into the chair, and lit another cigarette. He sat scowling. Who was the kid? Where did he come from? The same questions applied to Drew Dodge, didn't they? And maybe the answers for one would fit the other. Only Dodge would never give them now. And where was the kid? How could someone so young come from the far past? Dodge's past. What was it? A bad start left behind somewhere, a new life begun far away. Here. Dodge's words to Owens had been *I wasn't even the same person then.* Maybe not. But whoever he was, he'd owned the same face. And that had worried him. No snapshots in an album on the coffee table. No photos with any of those newspaper clippings about him and his shopping mall. Then he'd gone on television, and the past had jumped to catch him up.

But kill him? It still made no sense. Dave swallowed his whisky, put out his cigarette, rose and went to the telephone. He poked the numbers of the Glass House in LA, and said to Jeff Leppard, "Do something for me, will you?"

"Morales says you're hotdogging up there," Leppard said. "Did you light at the Oaktree Inn as promised?"

"I did. Get the police in Seattle to send somebody smart around to talk to a woman named Virginia Hollywell. And ask her if she had a houseguest from Rancho Vientos staying with her lately. She may have been warned I'd be checking on her, so she may lie. Make sure Seattle verifies her story. Complete with dates."

"What for? Who the hell is this woman?"

"It would take too long to explain. But if her granddaughter Matilda wasn't with her, then maybe she was down in LA killing Drew Dodge. Please check it out."

"You saying it was a girl?" Leppard said.

"I don't know many boys named Matilda," Dave said. "I told Samuels the night I got knifed it might be a girl. And I thought so again when the kid shot at me and hit Samuels. It just might be. How is Samuels?"

"He's coming along okay," Leppard said. "You had Morales turn in one Murray Berman. I've got the sheriff's report on that. But it doesn't take us anywhere. We already knew what the kid looked like, the kind of car he drove."

"The gun is the point. Dodge had a gun and used it. Oh, I talked to Sonia White. She heard the gun go off, too. But she thought it was a backfire."

"She never mentioned any backfire to me."

"She forgot till I came along. What's this about jurisdiction in the Dodge case? The sheriff blocking you from working out there?"

"Don't pretend you mind," Leppard said. "Just red tape. Judge will fix it tomorrow. Meantime, the sheriff has to share what he gets with me, only he isn't trying."

"Nobody up here cares about Drew Dodge anymore."

"Only you. Don't get yourself killed, okay? Remember, this one is armed and dangerous."

"I remember," Dave said. "It's Drew Dodge's gun, I expect. The kid must have taken it off his body. Dodge bought it the day after he talked with the kid at home."

"You're on top of it, all right." Leppard's voice held grudging admiration laced with annoyance. "How did you get that letter Berman wrote Dodge? Out of Dodge's files, right? You entered the house without permission, while the family was at the funeral."

"Letters were blowing on the wind today," Dave said. "There was a beauty from one of our distinguished Sacramento lawgivers. But I'll tell you about that after you hear from Seattle. Hell, I even have a letter from the kid."

"Jesus. You know where to find him?"

"There's no return address," Dave said.

The food in the Oaktree Inn restaurant was better than he expected. He liked watching a log fire burn while he ate a veal and mushroom concoction in a cream, butter, and wine sauce. The list of California wines had good labels on it. He chose a Rutherford *liebfraumilch*. The Scotches in his room had picked him up and made him hungry. The food and wine left him ready to sleep. A good thing, since he hated watching television by himself, and there was no decent music to listen to, and he had no wish to read travel magazines. He began shedding his clothes almost before the door of his unit shut behind him. He yanked back the covers on the wide bed, went into the bathroom, reached for the shower handles, and the telephone burred. It was on the wall by the shaving mirror. He took it down and said "Brandstetter" into it.

"I left messages." It was Tom Owens. He didn't sound right. "Why haven't you returned my calls?"

"I got Mel Fleischer's information from Larry," Dave said. "I thought that was what it was about. Larry said—"

"Listen to me, Dave. I'm a hostage."

Dave squinted. "What was that word?"

"Hostage. In a trailer on the beach. In a cove three miles north of the Rancho Vientos turnoff. We're at a pay phone now. He says the only way he'll let me go is if you come to the trailer. Alone. No police."

Dave sat down on the closed toilet. "The tall, thin kid with long hair?"

"He was watching us at the church. From the hills. But he was too far off. The change of cars confused him. He followed the BMW thinking you were in it. He forced me off the road, and—wait, let go!"

The phone clattered. "Tom?" Dave called. "It's okay. Tell him I'll come. Right away. I'm sorry about this."

"Don't come!" Owens shouted. "He'll kill you, Dave."

The connection broke. Dave stared at the receiver, listened to it hum. His heart was thudding. He hung up the phone, put his clothes back on, the trenchcoat, the tweed hat, and went out into the cold and wet to find Morales. He moved along a sheltered walkway, looking at parked cars till the lights of one near the end. Morales rolled down the window and sneezed. He held a big paper cup of coffee and he looked miserable. "I thought you were in for the night," he said, and sneezed again. "Damn."

"Did you draw this assignment for life?" Dave said.

"It's fascinating." Morales wiped his nose with a crumpled handkerchief. "I wouldn't miss it." He set the coffee on the dashboard and started the engine. "Where are we going now?"

"I'm going to Thousand Oaks. I checked with my answering service. Apex Insurance Agency needs me. Now. An auto crash that might be suicide." Dave pushed back the cuff of his trenchcoat to see his watch. "It's only eight. I should be back by midnight." He held out his Oaktree Inn key. "That's a rotten cold you've got. Go on in, crawl into bed, get warm. There's no need for you to follow me."

Morales's eyelids were heavy as he searched Dave's face. "I wish to hell I could believe you."

"It's out of the danger zone. I'll be okay."

"No way." Morales shook his head, sneezed again, twice, blew his nose again. "What kind of police officer do you take me for? I'm here to protect you." He shuddered. "I'm going to protect you."

"Well, at least take a hot bath. I'll fix you a stiff drink. Go on like this, you'll get pneumonia."

Morales tried to answer but coughed instead, a rough, deep cough that brought tears to his eyes. He stared, and gasped out, "A hot bath? Oh, boy." He pushed open the car door, tottered out, locked the door. He turned Dave a pitiful smile. "Lead me to it," he said.

The coast road lay deserted in the night and the rain. The rain fell harder here on the ocean side of the hills, wind off the ocean driving it in gusts. Dave swung onto the highway and headed north, an eye on the odometer. The windshield wipers batted away the steady wash of rain down the curved glass in front of him. The headlights bored yellow through the rain, which sometimes blew in slanting sheets. Even though the windows were closed, he could hear the crash of the surf off to his left. Its weight shook the roadway. He could feel it thud and thud. *It was a dark and stormy night.* He smiled thinly to himself.

At three miles, he slowed. The guardrail to keep cars from going over the sharp drop to the beach was white and he could see it faintly. But he saw no gap in it anywhere wide enough to admit a car. Yet the distance had to be right—the kid wanted Dave to come and be killed. The kid must have hauled his trailer down onto the beach by an access Dave had already passed, or one that lay ahead. The kid wanted Dave to come to the trailer on foot. He shrugged, swung the Jaguar around, parked it on the road shoulder. He groped a flashlight out of the glove compartment, got out into the lashing rain, dropped the flashlight into the left-hand pocket of the trenchcoat, where it balanced the weight of Morales's police special in the right-hand pocket. He had lifted the revolver quietly from the holster Morales had hung on the bathroom doorknob when he stepped into the steaming tub.

Dave's SIG Sauer seemed always to lie in that pine drawer on the sleeping loft. He never had it with him when he needed it.

He locked the car, walked along beside the guardrail to the break, shone the flashlight downward. The feet of swimmers, surfers, picnickers had worn a narrow path into the steep face of the bank. It trickled rainwater. Dave stepped down onto it cautiously, and made his way, bracing himself with a hand against the crumbly bluff face, down to the beach. Clumps of rough rock jutted out of the sand here. He shone the light around, looking for a trailer. And not finding it. High rocks shelved out ahead of him. Maybe around behind them he'd find the trailer. Tucked out of sight from the road. A place to hide. A place to hold a hostage.

He plodded, head down, through the sucking sand, making for the outcrop, and finding the rushing surf washing over his shoes. Where the rocks reached into the tide, the waves crashed over them. If he was going to get across, he was going to get wet—no way out of that. He studied the timing of the waves in the beam of the flashlight for a minute. Then he pushed the flashlight away and made a dash for it. He twisted an ankle, scraped a knee, but he made it to the other side of the promontory. The trenchcoat was heavy. His shoes squished. He shivered with cold.

He didn't want to shine the flashlight here, and he didn't have to. A light burned in the trailer. Dim behind a curtain, but there. Probably a camper's lamp. The trailer was no more than a hulk of blackness. The car, too. Not hitched to the trailer, standing behind it on the sand. Dave crouched and groped on the sand for stones. He didn't find any. He moved on a few steps, crouched again, and had better luck. He started for the trailer, and the door opened. Blue-white light streamed out into the rain. The figure of the tall, skinny kid stood there. He squinted against the dark. The light behind him caught and shone in his long fair hair. A pistol hung in his hand.

"He ain't here," he said. "Where the fuck is he?"

Someone answered from inside, but Dave couldn't make out the words. The door slammed shut. It made a tinny sound. The trailer was metal. The rain made a racket, beating on the trailer. It would be noisy inside. Add that to the noise of the wind and the surf, and a crowd could arrive out here and not be heard. He trudged to the trailer and put his ear to the cold, wet siding. The kid was shouting. "Why did you have to go and say I was gonna kill him, you God damn fool? I should have shot you like I said I'd do, right there at the phone. He ain't a-comin' for you. So what good are you to me?"

Again, Dave couldn't hear Tom Owens's answer.

"No good, that's what. I'm gonna have to shoot you anyways. You seen my face." Footsteps shook the trailer, the door yanked open again. The light fell out into the rain. Dave stepped back into darkness. The boy began to wail now. "I don't know how the Lord Jesus could let this happen to me. I never done nothin' in my life but look for my daddy. I never meant to kill nobody, now it looks like there ain't no end to it. Why? Why did he have to draw a gun on me?"

Three metal steps went down from the trailer door to the sand. Dave heard the steps rattle now. He took another step back into the dark. The boy's keening voice came on the wind from out on the beach. "Him that run out on my mom and me sixteen year ago. And her dyin' of drink, grievin' for him. A rich millionaire. And for all our pain and sufferin' and dyin' he ain't goin' to pay one nickel. No. He's goin' to get this big-time detective after me, and run me off."

The raving voice came and went. Dave dodged a quick look. The kid was walking in circles on the sand, waving his arms. "And when I says if he don't pay me I'm a-gonna tell all the wickedness he done back in Arkansas, damn if he don't pull out this here gun. On his own little boy that's been a-searchin' and a-seekin' for him all these years." Footsteps crunched in the wet sand. The boy ran up the steps. The trailer door banged shut. But the unstoppable words came through the walls. "And he fired that gun, Mr. Owens. Jesus is my witness. Fired off that gun right past my ear. What was I supposed to do, Mr. Owens?" The boy's voice broke into choking sobs. "My own daddy tried to kill me." He wept hard for a minute. Then, suddenly, he said, "Brandstetter ain't comin'. He don't care if I kill you. And I don't know what else to do."

Dave stepped out and threw a stone at the trailer door. The door flew open, and the kid fired wildly into the dark. Dave yanked Morales's gun from his pocket, and thumbed back the hammer. "Drop it!" he shouted. The boy swung and fired at him. He heard the whine of the bullet. He raised Morales's gun and squeezed the trigger. The gun kicked. The shot was loud. The boy's thin body gave a jerk, took a half turn, and pitched out onto the sand.

20

MAX ROMANO'S PLACE was quiet. It was early. In the small, dark-paneled bar, a handful of commuters hung on, clinking ice in glasses, and swapping stories, reluctant to face the rain-slick streets, the gridlocked freeways. From the kitchen came good smells, the muted rattling of pans and the banging of oven doors. The dining room tables with their snowy linen, neatly laid-out silver, crystal glinting in candlelight were vacant. Except for Dave's table in its corner under a stained-glass panel. Here he worked on a double Manhattan, and tried to improve Ken Barker's temper. The bulky police captain drank Old Crow, and glowered at Dave with eyes the color and coldness of gunmetal.

"We put out money and effort to protect you. And you act like a hotshot high school kid. You could have been dead on that beach. Washed out to sea. We could still be looking for you."

"Better me than Morales," Dave said. "Samuels was enough, Ken. I couldn't let that happen twice. Protecting me was your idea, remember. I never wanted it."

"You made that plain," Barker growled. "But Morales is still in trouble. For the worst mistake an officer can make—letting his gun be taken away from him."

"Gary Dean Duval is as crazy as they come," Dave said.

The kid was under double guard in the hospital ward of the county jail near Rancho Vientos. The bullet from Morales's gun had shattered a bone in his upper right arm. He had lost blood while Dave crouched over him on the sand and Tom Owens drove the Jaguar to that public phone he'd used earlier to summon Dave. Dave had laid blankets from the trailer over the kid, but he'd gone into shock before the ambulance arrived. He was out of trouble now. He'd live. "He came out shooting. I knew he would. I wasn't putting Morales in his line of fire."

"You interfered with a police officer in the performance of his duty," Barker said stubbornly. "If Abe Greenglass wasn't your lawyer, I'd nail you for that."

"Samuels may never be the same," Dave said. "If you get off his case, all Morales has is a bad cold."

Barker's mouth twitched, but he didn't answer. He picked up Max's big menu and studied it through glasses with heavy horn rims. "Samuels doesn't hold what happened to him against you. You're oversensitive." Barker lowered the menu. "I do not think." He raised the menu again, and said from behind it, "When are you going to stop being a pain in the butt to me? When are you going to retire?"

"Maybe when you do." Dave took a brown envelope from inside his jacket, and laid the envelope in front of Barker. "Somebody official ought to do something with that. And Jeff Leppard isn't speaking to me, won't let me near him, won't return my calls."

"Smart kid." Barker picked up the envelope, untucked the flap with thick fingers, peered inside. "What is this stuff? Bank statements?"

"And a letter." Dave told Barker about Bud Hollywell. "I'd have put it in the hands of the local district attorney but I don't know him. I don't know where his loyalties lie. I thought if LAPD gave it to the State's Attorney here, and he turned it over officially to the man up there, something useful might happen."

Barker grunted. "Something had better." He pushed the envelope into his pocket. "I'll see to it. Thanks."

"Now you tell me something," Dave said. "What was in those manila envelopes in Duval's trailer?"

"Aha. Now we get to the real reason for all this." Barker gestured at the handsome, shadowy room. "You don't prize my company. You just lured me here to pump me." He showed his teeth in a kind of smile, and laid the menu down. "Okay. Pay for it. I'll have the Maine lobster and filet mignon."

Dave said, "Hell, you can get that anywhere. Let me tell you about Max's scaloppine, his incomparable—"

Barker said, "I'm ordering it for the price."

Dave grinned. "Tell me about those envelopes."

"There was the kid's birth certificate," Barker said. "Barely readable, I understand. Wine spills, coffee stains. But his mother was May Ellen Stubblefield, his father was Henry Arthur Duval."

"Same initials as Harold Andrew Dodge," Dave said.

"He had documents of his own, Dodge did." Barker took a swallow of his drink. "They're fakes, the sheriff says, but he hasn't traced where they came from yet."

"But he was the same man?" Dave lit a cigarette.

"The fingerprints on record with the California Department of Motor Vehicles match those of Duval the police have in Hackett, Arkansas, the last place he served time."

"For those "wickednesses" the kid was going to tell about unless Dodge paid him?"

Barker made a face. "Dodge was in and out of jails all over the Deep South for check-kiting and various confidence games. He had the good looks that cause silly women to fall over themselves to trust him with their money."

"And silly men," Dave said, "Dodge himself at the head of the line. He could have grown a beard, couldn't he, but he wouldn't hide those looks. So he settled for not letting himself be photographed. It wasn't enough."

"He was vain, all right. Did you know—he wasn't thirty-five, he was forty-two." Barker smiled wryly, shook his head, and finished off his Old Crow. "The kid was born in 1970, and Duval didn't stay around much longer. May Ellen became an alcoholic and part-time prostitute. Somebody right out of Tennessee Williams, mooning over her lost love. She hung onto every scrap of newsprint about his checkered career while they were together, read them over and over year after year till they're falling apart. Dragged little Gary Dean all over the map, trying to find his dad. And when she was dying of cirrhosis, she made the kid swear on the Bible that he'd never stop looking."

"And he never did," Dave said. "Photographs?"

"Clipped from the papers. Also snapshots. Gary Dean must have studied them. He sure as hell knew his daddy when he saw him on the TV in that Venice bar. High school pictures. Wedding pictures. Baby pictures. Picnics. A canoe trip. Up until Daddy walked out of that jail in Hackett, Arkansas, when nobody was looking."

"And all the way to California and a shiny new life."

"Shiny and short," Barker said. "Ah, here's Max."

The rain was only a drizzle this noon, but steady. The splintery old pier was deserted except at its far end, where a solitary brown-skinned woman bundled in sweaters under a yellow slicker and sou'wester patiently held a long fishing pole, and leaned on the white wooden rail, a bucket at her rubber-booted feet. Dave passed the carousel where the orgatron wheezed, drummed, clashed its mechanical cymbals for no visible ears, where the sleekly lacquered horses rose and fell on their brass poles, and the mirrors framed in gilt and crimson flashed back the pewter light of the dreary day. Nobody rode.

The booths were shut up behind scarred, painted plywood—the baseball toss, the dart throw, the shooting gallery. No one wandered the creaky aisles of the penny arcade. The gypsy lady automaton in her glass box gazed blankly at the rain from under her faded purple satin turban. At her back, electronic games flickered fitfully and beeped, begging quarters from absent pockets. In their tall, metal-raftered pavilion, the bumper cars in carnival blues, reds, yellows, squatted in disarray. Nobody rode.

But a white-painted outdoor lunch counter was open. The flaking tin sign above it read FRIED SHRIMP HAMBURGERS HOT DOGS. Rain wept down the letters. Dave smelled the grease and onions before he reached the counter. Chrissie sat there in a plastic hooded raincoat on a rusty stool, shrimp and french fries in an oval red plastic basket in front of her, coffee steaming in a wax-paper cup, a paper napkin crumpled in a fist. Her white cane with the red tip hung off the edge of the counter, and she looked about as cheerful as the weather. Dave said, "Friends are always recommending unpretentious little places to eat nobody knows about." He climbed onto a stool next to her. The stool creaked and tottered. "Where the food is scrumptious. Is the food here scrumptious?"

"Thank you for coming." For a minute her face lit up with a smile. Her eyes were hidden behind dark glasses. But they wouldn't have lit up anyway. "No." She poked with a thin, nail-bitten finger at the shrimp and chips. "Not scrumptious. I only ordered so he'd let me sit here and wait for you." She pushed the basket in Dave's direction. "You want to eat them so they don't go to waste?"

"I'll pass, thanks. Chrissie, I would have come and collected you. There's no reason to sit out in this weather."

"The reason is," she said, "that he'd never look for me here. He knows I hate the pier." The sea moved under the planks beneath them. The massive old pier stakes shuddered. "The noise, and all the people bumping into you. He brought me here once. It panicked me. I try not to let that happen. I'll learn. But I haven't learned yet. Anyway, it's the last place he'd look for me."

"And why shouldn't he look for you?"

"Because—I had to see you alone. Mr. Brandstetter, this is terrible." Without thinking, she groped for the basket and began to eat. Mouth full of shrimp, she said, "You're going to think I'm a real bitch."

Dave laughed. "I guess not. What's the matter?"

"You're going to think"—she chewed, swallowed, gulped coffee—"I'm the most ungrateful person that ever lived on this earth." Tears leaked down her face.

"Come on, Chrissie." Dave pulled napkins from a corroded dispenser on the counter and wiped the tears. "If you believed that, you wouldn't have called me."

"It had to be you. There's nobody else." She sniffled, took the napkins from Dave, wiped her nose, and stuffed her mouth with chips. She sat dolefully chewing for a minute, got the mouthful down, and cried to him, "You're his best friend. I can't tell him myself. You have to tell him for me. Please?"

"Tell him what?" Dave said.

"That I don't want to be married to him anymore," she wailed. "I don't want to be married to anyone. I'm too young. I have to finish growing up first. He is the kindest, gentlest person in the world. And I hate myself for this. He saved my life. I mean, you don't find people like that in real life. Only in books."

"He's real, Chrissie," Dave said.

"I know, and that's why I feel so awful. I can't bear to hurt him. I can't bear it." She began crying hard now, choking the words out. "I shouldn't have let him do it. But I couldn't see any way out, to escape from Brenda and Ken Kastouros and foster homes and all that. And he said, 'If you're married, you're your own woman, nobody can harm you, I'll protect you, Chrissie.' And it wasn't right"—she groped out to touch Dave's arm now—"but I was in a panic and I said yes. And he loved me and—and—and I let him think—think—"

"I know what he thought," Dave said. "You're right. You did the wrong thing. But so did he. He was older. He should have known better. He didn't love you, Chrissie. He played that part because he thought you loved him."

"Oh, God." Chrissie stared at him, mouth open. "Is that true? You're not just making it up?"

"Somebody has to tell the truth around here," Dave said. "I've been trying to get him to tell you because it was the only thing to do, the only honest, decent thing to do. But he was afraid of hurting you."

"I bore him," she said. "I know it's just so boring for him to be around me, to have me depending on him and being so young and he knows so much and I don't know anything yet. And he's so kind and so patient and—"

"He'll be all right. What's going to happen to you?"

"The Chapmans want to adopt me," Chrissie said, "or have me as a foster child till I'm twenty-one."

"That could be rough on Dan'l," Dave said. "You know he loves you very much." She turned to him, surprise on her face. Dave said, "I know you think he's just a child, but he doesn't think of himself that way. And you are very beautiful and very sweet. Having you there under the same roof—"

"I don't know what I'll do," she said flatly, "but I can't go on doing what I've been doing to Cecil." She tugged at Dave's coat sleeve. Urgently. "You will tell him for me, won't you? I just can't."

"You can." Dave got off the stool. "And you will. Come on. Let's go find him."

"But you said on the phone you had a plane to catch," she cried. "Some assignment in Denver."

Dave laughed, helped her off the stool, put the cane in her hand, and offered her his arm to walk her back up the pier. "From now on," he said, "I'm through catching planes." To the beat of their heels on the massive old planks, he almost started whistling in the rain.

Continue reading for a preview of the next
Dave Brandstetter novel

OBEDIENCE

1

HE WAS QUITTING. But notifying all the insurance companies in the West he'd done death claims investigations for in recent years turned out to be a long job. He had sat down to do it after lunch, and was still typing away in a lonely little island of lamplight in the looming, raftered room when Cecil Harris walked in at midnight. A field reporter for television news, the tall, lanky young black lived with Dave. He ambled down the room, glanced over Dave's shoulder as he passed the desk, hung his jacket on the hat tree, and rattled glasses and bottles at the bar.

"I didn't mean for you to work so hard," he said. "Let me put that on our computer. You only need to write one letter. Give me the list of addresses. Send the same letter everyplace, just a different salutation each time."

Dave ground a finished sheet wearily out of the little typewriter, laid the page aside with its envelope, closed the case of the portable, put it into a deep lower drawer of the desk, and closed the drawer. He ached between the shoulder blades. "They'd know it was a form letter."

"There's a daisy-wheel printer in the program director's office. I can use it at night." Cecil handed Dave a Glenlivet on ice in a stocky glass. "Daisy-wheel printer—nobody would know it wasn't typed."

"I'd know," Dave said. "And no one deserves to be treated that way." He took off the glasses he used for reading and writing, and laid them on the desk. "Not even insurance executives." He stood, stretched, picked up his cigarettes and lighter from the desk, and carried these, with his drink, to the corduroy couch that faced the fireplace. He dropped onto it. Cecil sat down beside him and Dave put a light kiss on his mouth. "Thanks for the offer."

"Hell," Cecil said, "I was the one who talked you into it." For months, he had been asking Dave to quit. Dave's balking had been partly play-acting, but Cecil hadn't seen that, and now he was feeling guilty. He gave Dave a worried glance. "Up to me to try to make it easy, if I can."

"Don't sweat it," Dave said. "I'll work it out." He tasted the scotch, and lit a cigarette. "Why not look at it this way? I was sharpening my typing skills. To write my memoirs, right?" Cecil moaned. Dave changed the subject. "And what did you do today?"

Cecil took a breath. "Down in San Pedro County, there's a place I bet you never heard of. The Old Fleet Marina." It had been there twenty-five years. Dave had heard of it, had even been there sometime, though he forgot why. But he didn't say this. Cecil sipped brandy, hummed gratefully at the taste, leaned his head back. "Half-dead factories and warehouses all around, windows smashed out. Oil derricks. Wobbly docks, posts all crusty with barnacles below the water. Water dark and greasy. Crowd of old boats, rusting away, rotting away. Some don't even have motors."

"A floating junkyard?" Dave said.

Cecil shook his head. "Home. People living on those boats." He sat forward, elbows on knees, turning the brandy snifter in long fingers, watching it glumly. "Been living there for years, some of them."

"And you drove down there with a camera crew?"

Cecil nodded. "Four this afternoon."

"What was the lead?" Dave said.

"The boat folks are being ousted. In sixty days. And most of them don't have the money to lease mooring spaces at good marinas."

"The good ones have waiting lists years long anyway," Dave said. "And they don't allow living on board."

"Right. The Old Fleet was the only one that did, and the only cheap one. But, even if there was another, those with no engines—they'd have to be towed there, and towing comes expensive." He shook his head, gloomily drank from the snifter. "Money sure can make people heartless."

"It's a five-thousand-year-old trend," Dave said. "Who has the money this time?"

"Name of Le Van Minh," Cecil said. "A Vietnamese importer. Lives here. Residency permit. He's owned the place for years. Now developers want to buy it, gentrify it, build condos all around, fancy restaurants and shops. The Old Fleet boaties are protesting. The protest was the news story, really. But they're poor. They can't win."

Dave said, "They probably couldn't win if they were rich." He snuffed his cigarette, knocked back the rest of his scotch, set down the glass. "These days, you see something you want—factory, fast-food outlet, supermarket chain—and you've got the money, you get it, regardless of how the owner feels. It's called a hostile takeover." He pushed up off the couch. "Don't ask me to explain it."

"I don't guess Le minds selling," Cecil said. "He just owns it. I don't think it means anything to him. Just another investment. Don't suppose he ever saw it. Boat folks claim he only just heard there were people living there."

Dave winced and rubbed the back of his neck. "Dave, the demon typist, is tired," he said.

"Let's go to bed," Cecil said.

Dave walked in from the brick courtyard, the taste of coffee and blueberry muffins lingering in his mouth. He had just seen Cecil off to work in his flame-painted, blue-carpeted van. It was September, staffers were taking late vacations, Cecil was working double shifts this week. Dave ought to have factored that into his retirement plans. He had counted on Cecil's company during the days. Living alone he had never liked. He lit a cigarette, and leaned in the doorway, studying the room. Books had stacked up on the floor, against the pine plank walls. Books cluttered the brick surround of the fireplace, the desk and bar at the far end of the long room, the golden oak mission-style library table that stood behind the couch.

He had lived for years in this strange place on Horseshoe Canyon Trail—the two main buildings had started as stables, and in damp weather still smelled faintly of horse. But though Amanda, his very young stepmother, had put up open sleeping lofts here, had modernized the cookshack, installed clerestory windows and split-leveled the floor of the front building, Dave himself hadn't marked the place much. He'd been too busy. He had bought Navajo rugs for this building, some Mexican pottery pieces for the front building, but he'd never hung any pictures, and he liked pictures. He liked tall bookcases, too, but the only ones here he'd slapped up back by the desk when he first moved in.

Well, now he wasn't busy anymore, was he? He had time to build all the bookshelves he wanted. This morning, while Cecil showered, Dave had signed, sealed, and stamped the letters, bundled them with a rubber band, and walked them out to the roadside box for the mailman to take away in his red, white, and blue jeep. Dave had made it official. The rest of his life was his own. And the first days of it, he was going to give to bookshelves and pictures—those watercolors by Larry Johns he'd bought last year, nice, loose, sure-handed sketches of the surf, rocks, dunes around the handsome beach house Johns shared with Tom Owens. Owens was an architect whose life Dave had saved a couple of times—the last time, because he'd put it in jeopardy.

He smiled grimly to himself, walked down the room and stood, head tilted, sizing up the long, knotty pine walls that flanked the fireplace. He liked the notion of bookshelves over, under, and around the windows. He turned, decided the pictures would look happiest lined up along the wall under the north sleeping loft. There was better height for the shelves on the fireplace wall. How many shelves? He had bought the lumber when he bought the place. It lay under blue plastic sheets sheltered by a vine-grown arbor at the back of the property. If termites and dry rot hadn't eaten it, there were probably enough board feet there. Dave needed a yardstick. Full of cheerful purpose, he started for the cookshack, where the tools were kept. And stopped.

A young woman stood in the doorway. He blinked at her. She carried a case, but he didn't think there was anything for sale in it. She was freckle-faced and sandy-haired, and wore a shirtmaker dress of crisp oyster-white twill with a floppy green bow at the throat. Her green-rimmed glasses were owlish, and she was doing her best to look prim and businesslike. He took her for a lawyer.

"Mr. Brandstetter," she said, "I'm Tracy Davis. Maybe you remember me. I used to work for Mr. Greenglass." She held out a business card. He went to her and took it, patted his shirt pocket, and remembered he'd left his reading glasses with the morning paper in the cookshack. Maybe the way he squinted at the card told her he couldn't read it. "Public Defender," she said, "San Pedro County. I need your help."

"Sorry." He held up both hands, took a backward step. "You're too late. As of this morning, I've retired."

The light went out of her face. "Oh, no."

"Don't feel bad," he said. "There are plenty of good investigators around." He started for his desk. "Come in. I'll write down some names and numbers for you."

She followed him. "It's not that. The Public Defender's office has its own investigators."

5

He sat at the desk, opened a drawer, brought out his address book. "Then what are you doing here?"

"I need the best," she said.

"That's very flattering but"—he shook his head—"what kind of retiree would I be if I only lasted one day at it? Would you respect a man like that?"

"I asked Mr. Greenglass to recommend someone, and he said you were the only choice. I've read about you in *Time, Newsweek, People*. Seen you on Ted Koppel, Oprah Winfrey, Phil Donahue. You're the best." She frowned. "Is it your health? You don't look sick."

"I'm fine." Dave switched on the desk lamp, found a pen, and, squinting to make out street and phone numbers, wrote them on the back of the card she'd given him. "But I won't be fine if I go back to work. I've been stabbed and shot, beaten up, burned out, half drowned, and run off roads too often lately. I'm tired of hospitals." He handed her the card. "My reflexes are slowing down, and everything ugly is speeding up. It's time I quit."

"But Mr. Greenglass promised me," she wailed. "If you don't save Andy Flanagan, no one will. No one else can."

"What makes Andy Flanagan so hard to save?"

"The man they say he killed is Vietnamese," she said, "and Andy lost his arm in Nam. And everyone who knows him knows he hates those people. To this very day. Thirteen years later. He is not a winning man. He's surly, full of hate and self-pity. He's a bigot and a bully."

"We don't put people in jail for those things." Dave stood up. "What's the evidence?"

She laughed hopelessly. "Oh, God. Where do I begin?"

"How about over a cup of coffee?" Dave said. "Cookshack is across the courtyard, there." He walked toward the sunlit front doorway. She followed.

"What lovely rugs," she said. "Does this mean you'll take the case?"

"It means I'll listen to you," he said, "because I don't think anybody is going to shoot me for that. At least not right away."

Her heels rattled across old bricks scattered with the curled, dry leaves of the oak that spread its branches over the courtyard. "Listen and advise?" she wondered.

"Possibly." He pulled open the cookshack screen door and held it so she could duck inside under his arm. "But not consent," he said. Morning sunlight through tall windows dappled with leaf shadows the yellow enamel of cupboards. "Sit down." He waved a hand at a scrubbed deal table surrounded by plain pine chairs, and began putting together coffeemaker and coffee at a stately old nickel-plated range that cunningly hid the latest gadgetry. "You drove a long way to get here. You hungry?"

"Just coffee, please. No food." She pulled out a chair, sat down, slipped her shoulder bag off, and set it with the attaché case on the floor. "I'm too upset."

Dave took mugs down from a cupboard, spoons from a drawer. "New at this, are you?" He brought mugs, spoons, napkins to the table. "This your first homicide?"

She gave a bleak laugh. "I wish it were. But Andy Flanagan's my half-brother. He was a gentle, timid kid. Back then. The war changed him. None of the family wants anything to do with him now." Her eyes behind the big lenses pleaded up at him. "It's why I came to you. Andy is all mouth. He wouldn't kill anybody. At bottom he's a coward."

"He lost an arm in combat," Dave said.

"And he has a purple heart to prove it." She used that bleak laugh again, and bent to dig cigarettes and a green throwaway lighter from her bag. "But you can buy purple hearts at pawnshops."

Dave went back to the stove, brought the coffeemaker to the table, and poured coffee into the mugs while she lit her cigarette. The smoke smelled good. He found his own cigarettes and lighter lying with his glasses on the folded copy of the morning *Times*. He frowned at the paper. He'd read only the entertainment section this morning, curious about a citywide music festival that yesterday had honored John Cage, whom he'd known long ago. He hadn't

JOSEPH HANSEN

read the news—not even the headlines. He picked up the cigarettes, went back to the table, sat down. "When did this killing happen?"

"A little before midnight." She blew smoke away, tasted her coffee. "At the Old Fleet Marina."

Dave stared, the flame of his lighter halfway to his cigarette. "A Vietnamese?"

"Le Van Minh. The man who owns the place."

Dave lit the cigarette and put the lighter down. "I understood he hardly knew where it was."

"If he didn't," she said, "Andy Flanagan told him."

"Flanagan lives there? He's one of the boat people?"

"The one making the most noise," she said. "I don't know that the rest of them agree—they're an odd bunch—but he claims he's their spokesman."

"What did Flanagan do—telephone Le?"

"He wanted a summit meeting." She drank some coffee, turned ash off her cigarette in a big, square clear-glass ashtray. "All he or any of them at the Old Fleet had seen were lawyers handing them vacate notices and deadlines. Andy wanted to talk to the man himself." She gave her head a sorry shake. "He'd once told the others that if Le didn't back down, he'd kill him. Whose country was this, anyway? What had we fought a war for—so a damn Slant could turn Americans out of their homes?"

"I'm surprised Le came. At night? Alone? It's no place for a stranger—not as I remember it."

"Especially not a well-dressed stranger," she said, "driving a large, expensive car. But the lawyers weren't with him. He didn't call them. His son Hai wanted to drive him. But Le wouldn't hear of it. And in a Vietnamese household, the father's word is law."

Dave nodded. "Filial piety," he said. "Obedience. Did he and Flanagan meet?"

"Andy waited on his boat. The appointment was for eleven. And when Le hadn't come on board by midnight, Andy

8

went to ring him again. At the pay phone on the pier. And stumbled over his body."

"Who called the police?"

"Andy, once he'd got over his shock. It's the only defense he's got. He knew he'd be arrested. But he phoned the police anyway."

"What options did he have?" Dave said. "It would have been stupid to run."

She took a last drag from her cigarette, snubbed it out, blew the smoke away, and gave him a grave and steady look. "Maybe not—not if you won't help him."

"I should have moved to a remote cottage on the Sussex downs and kept bees," he said.

She frowned, tilted her head. "What?"

He sighed. "I'll look into it." Her face lit up, and he lifted a hand. "Abe Greenglass has been my lawyer for a lifetime. He's gotten me out of some very serious scrapes and he's never asked anything of me before, so I'll look into this for you, but that's all. I don't promise to find anything. There may be nothing to find. Flanagan may be slyer than you think."

She shook her head. "He's a lot of things, but sly isn't one of them. You'll find something," she said.

Joseph Hansen (1923–2004) was the author of more than twenty-five novels, including the twelve groundbreaking Dave Brandstetter mystery novels. The winner of the 1992 Lifetime Achievement Award from the Private Eye Writers of America, Hansen was also the author of *A Smile in his Lifetime*, *Living Upstairs*, *Job's Year*, and *Bohannon's Country*. He was a two-time Lambda Literary Award-winner.